# The Road to Callamoon

*By* Crystal Rose Cline

# Chapter One

The moon shone through the autumn night, illuminating beauty and horrors alike; for among the leafless hardwoods and glimmering ponds, scraggly beasts of burden trod, drawing wagons over the wooded paths.

The wagons carried grain, weapons, tools and clothing, all wrenched from the hands and homes of those who owned them. Dragged behind the wagons were unbroken centaurs, elves, and faeries of red and pink wings held together by chains and rusty shackles—shackles made of shattered dreams.

All were under forty, most in their late teens and early twenties. Some of them had been as stubborn as a wild mule, some as compliant as a bit of clay. But under the punisher's whip they were all the same—broken of body and of spirit, knowing their fate and unable to fight it. Hopeless. Even the strongest bowed his head, counting the dirt as his equal.

But one elf refused to be broken. He acted with compliance, but stood with his head high and a holy fire glowing in his eyes. Words of hope spilled from his lips with every step he took. His only desire was to siphon hope into a pink-wing's heart.

"God is with us." He said. "He will not forsake you. He will give you what you need."

"But I am tired." She sobbed.

"He is rest for the weary. He will give you strength. Do not give up."

She could not give up. The wagon wouldn't be stopped till the sun rose. She could not rest before then.

But it was dark and the steady tug of the wagon on her body gave her no chance to recover as she tripped over a rock. She cried out, but the caravan would not be stopped. Her shins scraped against the ground as the rusty chains pulled her forward, too fatigued to pull herself back to her feet.

Strong arms scooped her up, the elf grunting with the effort. "Don't give up. He will carry you through."

"What are you doing?" The punisher shouted. "Put her down!"

But the elf still carried her. He could stand. He could walk. He could hope. She could not.

"Put her down!"

A strip of pain lit his back like burning fire. He paid no heed to it. He would not put her down. More stripes, welts, and cuts rose upon his back, deep green liquid oozing from the broken skin. His arms felt weaker and he heard the fairy's pleas to put her down. She could walk she said. He need not carry her. But he held her tighter and opened his mouth, pouring forth a song for all to hear.

*Praise Him in your trials*
*Praise Him all the while*
*He took up His cross*
*He paid the cost*
*Now it is your turn*
*For His love to burn*
*And praise Him in this storm*

The elves, their spirits less damaged by time than the faeries had been, added their glorious voices to the melody. A few faeries looked up. A few added their voices. A few gained hope.

The punisher's countenance shifted. The brilliance of the elf's flame, no matter its worth to society, would make him worthless at auction. He inflamed others with the intensity of his light. That light had to be put out.

The elf knew this, yet he stood tall and sang loud, promising to continue on with his song until the punisher dealt the death blow. He would glow, he would shine, and he would give everything he had to give if only it showed one creature The Way.

A silent *whoosh* passed beside the elf, followed by a dull *thunk* as body and head fell separate to the ground. Another *whoosh* and a second punisher lay dead. A black horse leapt among the shackled creatures and shattered their anchor before disappearing again into the night.

They were free. They were free! Who determined the direction of the ensuing flight could not be distinguished—no creature cared what direction they ran so long as their path led someplace far from the Gueritac's wagons. Free! Dreams and hopes sprouted again with such rapidity as to surpass the speed of the captives' feet. Oh praise God for the unseen ally!

But the ally had not left yet. They wouldn't be safe until the Gueritac gave up the chase and, though the Gueritac pursued their prize, they were cut down as the dark creature darted between and around them, always striking where they did not expect.

Only the leader knew the situation. He, Shodak, drove his horse past his men and overtook the fleeing captives. The figure appeared. He was ready. He blocked a blow and slashed with a second, catching resistance at the sword's tip before the illusive flash disintegrated.

He paused. He could see nothing but the glimmer of black liquid on his sword. A wolfish howl pierced the night.

Yes! He had waited years for this to come! He knew what to do next. He sheathed his swords and propped himself on his saddle, waiting.

There! A flash of movement. He leapt forward, catching the rider about the waist. It struggled, and the horse equally so, rearing and prancing about until both riders fell to the ground.

"Cease!" He called to his followers. "I have found a prize indeed! Come and see!" then he hissed into the creature's ear, uttering a truer phrase. "My revenge has come at last."

# Chapter Two

He picked up another stick and strained his eyes, trying to see inside the rusty lock. If only he could press the twig against the mechanism in just the right...

*Snap!*

The twig fell to the ground in two pieces. He tightened his fists, fighting the urge to jerk his arms apart. His strength could not break the chains. Loose rust itched like fire against the cuts from the first three times he had tried.

"God gave me the spirit of self-control." He said beneath his breath. "I will not lose my temper."

Correction. He would not lose his temper *again*.

Three times he had already lost his temper and three times sharp bits of rusty metal scraped his skin, causing thick green liquid to dribble down his arm and drip off his elbow. He could feel it now, still sticky upon his green-tinted skin.

Kaiya always said his temper could run a mile a minute when the occasion struck, and this occasion seemed on the verge of putting a lightning bolt through his head. He did not have his medicinal supplies. Those had been taken from him. His shirt had been stripped off and disappeared into one of the wagons. The only 'valuable' thing he had left was his ring, a piece of priceless jewelry he had carefully concealed in his hair. Only God had kept the Gueritac from finding it.

He picked up another stick, poking and prodding the lock mechanism. After reaching the southern part of Criseyde he'd heard of a legend known as Dark Angel. In battle she was unpredictable, faster than light and blending into the dark. To the elves she was a hero—to the faeries she was a ghost, a creature to be feared and respected. Regardless of her standing between the two species, her only known mission was to eliminate every Gueritac in Criseyde.

He never thought he'd need her help. He was on a mission trip. He expected only to need a Bible and an audience—though he brought his medicine bag and a few weapons anyways.

But the Gueritac caught them by surprise. He had been given no time to fight or flee. He had been separated from his weapons the moment he awoke, for his awakening had been a Gueritac shoving a rag in his mouth and hauling him outside.

Outside his heart broke a thousand times. All around him young children were ripped away from their mothers. Babes under a year old were left in their mother's arms, only to be sold as adoptive children to the barren. Their mothers would be sold as wet nurses to those who could not or did not wish to nurse. The elders and children alone were left in the village to starve the winter through and hope the neighboring tribes would be merciful. But how could they be merciful when the same fate had fallen on them?

He heard a gritty creak come from his fetter. His heart leapt. He pushed a little harder. Just a little farther...

*Snap!*

The twig splintered in his fingertips. He let it fall to the ground, fighting the anger which welled within his breast.

"Have you gotten it?"

He looked up. The eyes of a pink-winged fairy met his. Eyes filled with fear and desperation. He smoothed out his natural temper. "Not yet, Ipsah. But I will not give up."

Her shoulders fell, though it had not seemed they had the ability to fall any more. The faeries had been captured several days before he had, so their hope could be more easily shattered. He remembered a lovely violet-winged fairy, bound yet defiant. Would she have acquired the same broken demeanor if she had been bound for longer?

He raised his hands, but reconsidered and tucked a strand of hair behind his pointy ear. Now was not the time. He reached for another twig, finding one he thought to be stronger than the last one. But this time he held out a hand for the fairy.

"Here. It might be easier if I undo yours first. Watch what I do so you can take mine off."

She didn't hesitate, placing her hand in his. He stuck the twig into the lock and twisted, careful, slow. The stick weakened, bent, ready to break. "Please." He whispered. "Please…"

*Chink!*

The rusty metal fell from her wrist. She uttered a sob of relief, rubbing the swollen band of skin with her still-fettered hand.

"Praise God!" He exclaimed. But he wasted no time, pushing the stick into the other lock, twisting, hoping, praying…An urgent whisper broke his concentration.

"Hide! Someone is coming!"

*Snap!*

The twig splintered, falling to the ground in sharp fragments. He searched the ground for another twig, but the urgency made his hands slippery. The shackles pulled at him, yanking him after the group as they sought shelter behind sparsely clad saplings.

His heart beat faster. His fingers fumbled among decaying leaves. If only he could unlock her and spare her from being recaptured, he didn't care what happened to him. To spare one creature would be delight enough to last him many years of slavery.

"Do not fear!" A hoarse female voice called out. "I have come to free you."

A pause. Could they trust this newcomer? Silence prevailed a moment more, then rusty chains clinked and creaked as the fettered souls moved forward.

Ipsah clung to his arm, silent as death. He saw a sliver of hope in her eye. He had spent the past twenty hours reassuring her, telling her kind things and things about how God helped those who believed in Him. She had clung to his words, clung to him. Now her prayers were being answered. Did this newcomer know she was an answered prayer? Did she understand the hope she brought into the hearts of the wounded?

Then he saw her.

She held burning branches in her hand and pale gray eyes shone from her scarred face. Her body was thin and lithe, stringy black wings spreading out from her back. The scowl on her face reached all the way to her pointy ears. Faerie or elf? It didn't matter. She was beautiful.

He glanced at his fellow captives, but no one else seemed to be paying attention to the prettiness of her face. The only thing they saw was the slender piece of metal she held in her hand. A key.

"You. Hold out your hands."

Startled, he thrust his hands forward. She caught them by the shackles and inserted the key. The fetters fell from his wrists a grinding screech later. A few spots of green blood seeped anew from the jagged scratches his temper created, but the absence of rusty metal at his wrists was pure relief.

"Thank you."

"If you wish to thank me," she growled "find a healer and bid him to come with me."

"I *am* a healer."

"Good. We leave as soon as I unlock the last elf."

"What about the faeries?"

"I care not about them."

"I will not leave until *all* of these creatures are unshackled." He snapped. "Even if I have to do it myself."

He yanked a thick green stick from a sapling and turned to Ipsah. He pressed and twisted deliberately at the mechanism.

*Chink!*

The fairy's arms were immediately around his neck, grateful words jumbled together in her rush to get them out. All her pain seemed to have expanded to joy at such an explosive rate as to be both inexpressible and unintelligible.

"Calm down, Ipsah. You have nothing to fear. Neither God nor I would have forsaken you. God will never forsake you."

He patted her back, holding her in his arms. *Now* was the time. He unwound himself from her arms and reached into his hair, and pulling out his ring. "I want you to fly to Idlerose and find the queen. Tell her I need a recharge and I need to talk to her." He pressed his ring into her palm and let it rest, then pulled it away, a painted trillium tattooed on her hand. "Show her this, and she will know you came from me."

9

***

She watched the healer as he toyed with the pink-winged fairy's shackle. She heard a creak—so sweet to the ears of a captive—and the shackle dropped from the fairy's wrist. The fairy sobbed and embraced the elfin healer, words of gratitude spilling from her mouth like water over a falls.

The elf held her within his tender arms and whispered comforting words into her ear before taking a step back, out of her arms. He said something quiet, and the fairy kissed his cheek and thanked him one more time before flying off.

She stared after the fairy and at the elf, unable to remove her eyes while the moment still held. Normally, it would not have affected her to see an emotional display. Elves and faeries had emotions; it was a fact of life. A fact especially prominent on battlegrounds and among freed captives— places she had trodden for years.

But faeries and elves usually kept their distance, separated by the invisible brick walls of faerie hatred. This fairy knew no hatred and felt no walls. Her arms encircled him in such a way, one could easily be convinced she was encircling him with her heartstrings and would not ever let go.

This display captured not only her, but all present to witness it. Faerie, elf and centaur alike were spellbound by emotion. A few shed tears. A few placed their hand upon their hearts. A few more rubbed their arms, the cold having nothing to do with the shivers dancing upon their skin.

But she, a warrior, an unfeeling halfling, wished to reach out and let the elf hold *her* in his arms, for she knew he would hold her as tenderly as he had the pink-winged fairy. Her stomach burned and her heart jumped out of its rightful place. If only he would hold her for a little while...

Then the elf turned and the world released its breath. He moved toward a centaur, and it held out its hands, allowing the elf to unshackle him in the same fashion as he had the fairy. She turned, realizing she had not unlocked a fetter since the moment began, and found the nearest elf.

"Hands." She ordered. Then, inserting the key, she said "Tell me about the healer."

"Faelan?" The elf said. "He is from the north, near a place called Epidote. He is the best healer for many miles."

"Tell me about his relationship with the fairy."

"It is not much. A fairy died next to her before his capture, and they were unable to fit the healer anywhere else, so they put him by her. She was in hysterics. He comforted her and told her pretty things. He carried her when she was weak, though the punishers beat him for stepping out of place."

"Is he attached to her in any other way?"

"No."

"Thank you." She growled. "You are dismissed."

The elf bowed his head and moved away. She continued to the next creature and the next, removing their shackles with all the speed she possessed. All the speed she could summon under the circumstances.

Faelan. Yes, she owed this elf much. By breaking the prejudice in a single fairy he had given her the taste of emotion she had gone years without. For him she would release the faeries. For him she would treat them better in the future. Faelan deserved deep respect, and she would do everything in her power to ensure he received it.

***

Leaves crunched as his feet touched the ground, each leaf and twig distinguishable on his bare soles. He thanked the centaur who brought him and sent him on his way. But why did Warrior Girl come here?

The warrior girl's feet slammed into the ground nearby, a faint groan coming from her throat. Stunned, he ran to her side and grasped her elbow, pulling her to her feet.

"Are you alright?" he asked.

"No. Why would I have you come if I were alright? Come, I have healing supplies in the tent."

"What is wrong with you that you need me to fix?" He stopped her with a hand on her shoulder. He pulled it away again, a sticky black substance on his hand. "Is this—"

"Blood, yes." She said. "One gets injured often when they are in the business of freeing captives. But it is not a bad wound, comparative to some I have had."

"No matter." He replied, returning his hand to her shoulder. "Sit. I will find the supplies. Do you have a lamp?"

"Yes."

"Good. Stay put and I will gather them."

"Very well." She growled, lowering to a cross-legged position on the ground.

He heard dislike in her voice, though whether it was dislike of him or his orders he chose not to discover. His job was to heal her of body for now, of soul if possible. But first he needed the supplies.

He crawled into the tent, wide enough for two people to sleep comfortably with room in the far end for supplies. He spied the medicine bag and a lamp sitting dark beside it. Gathering those things, he glanced around, but did not see the final thing he needed. It could be in one of the closed bags, he did not know, but he also did not know how long the warrior girl had been bleeding. He could search for the book later.

The glow of a comfortable fire greeted him as he exited the tent. Warrior Girl sat beside the fire, her injuries freed of the black fabric she'd worn. Deciding it would be best not to ask questions, he used a burning stick to illuminate the lamp and set it behind Warrior Girl, expelling the shadows the one-sided fire had cast.

"It's not bleeding too badly. How long ago did you get it?"

"An hour and a half. I have been applying pressure since. I am not a novice at this, Healer Faelan. You need not baby me."

"I figured. I'm surprised you even needed me. In the process of getting these scars you probably learned how to treat every injury imaginable."

"I do not care what you think of my scars or potential curative abilities, Healer Faelan. I care only that my arm is patched up. Please begin."

He obeyed, mixing some yarrow leaf with a bit of water and setting it aside to soak. Then he took up the canteen and poured it over her wound. It was a deep gash stretching from her collarbone to her shoulder blade and around three-quarters of her arm. He pulled out the suture materials and a needle, carefully putting in a stitch and tying the knot before moving to the next. Stitches in place, he spread the yarrow paste over the wound and wrapped it in clean linen. Satisfied, he tucked the supplies away.

"Do you have any cheeses?"

"No. I have only some yogurt and bread. Why do you need it, Healer Faelan?"

"I do not, you do. You need something to help replenish your blood, and few things do as well as milk. Is it alright if I bleed your horse?"

"Do what you need, but do not kill her."

"You need not worry about that." He said. He filled a bowl with yogurt and took some blood from the vein on Warrior Girl's horse. He handed the bowl to Warrior Girl. "Drink."

She glared, but drank it down, leaving only a skim of pink residue in the bottom of the bowl. "Thank you Healer Faelan." She said, setting the bowl aside.

"Please," He said "Don't call me 'Healer Faelan.' Call me Faelan. But what should I call you?"

"You need not call me anything." She snapped. "Past tomorrow, you may never see me again."

"Ah, but you call me by my name. I must call you by yours."

Her lips stilled in an emotionless expression, her eyes seeming to concentrate on how the flame banished some small part of the darkness from the world while leaving the rest of the world in shadows. If only it could illuminate the entire world...

"My name is Angel." She said. "But I am not the Dark Angel of myth. I merely profit from the original halfling warrior's legacy."

"Halfling as in…"

"Half faerie, half elf. It is why my blood and wings are black. Faeries have red blood, elves have green. When mixed, they are black as night."

"I had not expected halflings to be as pretty as you." He said. "It is a pleasure to know you."

"Do not lie." She growled. "You care no more for me than a discarded twig or a rotten potato. Few creatures are tolerant of halflings."

"I don't care that you are a halfling. You are a creature of God, therefore I love you as much as any other."

She turned her head, her face expressionless again. "You are a handsome elf. Why do you waste your charm in trying to convince me of a lie?"

He dug into her eyes, pulling out the hidden emotions in her irises, seeing the pain, the loneliness, and the burning desire hidden deep within her hard heart. "Because I'm not lying."

She turned her face away. "I am waiting for someone to arrive. You should go to sleep. Help yourself to the tent. I will remain here—all night if necessary."

"Then we will both remain here. It will shorten the night if you have someone to talk to."

Her face reappeared with a strange watery glow in her eyes, like tears that would forever refuse to fall. "It is kind of you to offer, but I cannot ask such a thing of you."

"It was not an offer." He said, crossing his arms and taking a stubborn seat beside her. "I will remain here whether you like it or not. It will be a lot more pleasant, however, if you stop trying to get me to leave. It's a useless argument."

"Very well." She said, her eyes staring into the fire again. "Stay up as long as you like. I do not care."

But she did care. He could see it in her eyes.

# Chapter Three

A knock was heard against the thick door of the castle. The pink-winged fairy that made it shivered. It was late, she was weak. Perhaps her knocks would not be loud enough to wake the castle's inhabitants. She rubbed her arms, trying to build up warmth and courage enough to knock again.

Then she heard a creaking sound, slow and deep—a sound welcoming to the ears of one so chilled as she. Looking up, she saw a lone fairy pulling open the door, a bright ball of colors dancing in her hand and lighting her path.

"Come in." The fairy said, green eyes sparkling. "I've been waiting for you."

"But—"

"I know you did not think any messenger could have arrived faster than you. But I woke up hours ago, knowing you would arrive. Please, come in."

The fairy obeyed, her eyes stayed on the ground. The chill of the wind was soon cut off as the fairy closed the door and took her by the arm.

"Raise your head, dear. If you're going to be a Messenger you have to hold your head high. Come, sit by the fire."

The fairy looked up and saw a fire blazing on the hearth, inviting her to sit and pour out everything into its warmth, to let it cook until something delicious came from what could not be stomached before.

The fairy smiled at the upturned face and lead Ipsah to a warm chair. She took a seat opposite, her joyous face so much like the healer's in its demeanor that Ipsah could not help but love this violet-winged friend.

"My name is Kaiya, by the way. I probably should have mentioned that before. I'm technically the queen, but I'd prefer you didn't call me that. What's your name?"

"Ipsah."

"You have a lovely name, Ipsah. What brought you here?"

"He...he said to show you this." She said, holding out her palm so Kaiya could see the crimson-streaked trillium. "An elf named Faelan. He said he needs a recharge and to talk to you."

Kaiya leaned forward, fingering the trillium. Then she held a finger up, a bit of colored light dancing upon the tip. "Would you like me to get rid of it now you've delivered the message?"

Ipsah pulled her hand back. "No."

The fairy queen laughed. "I thought so. I just wanted to make sure." She laughed again, sparkles in her eyes. "He's a charming fellow, isn't he?"

Ipsah nodded.

"Where did you meet him? What do you think of him?"

"I like him very well." Ipsah said, her cheeks growing warm. "Is his character common among elves?"

"It depends on the tribe." Kaiya said. "He has spent a lot of time down in the South recently—a mission trip—and he's come across tribes that are perfectly ruthless. A few even threatened to tie him to a tree with his own entrails. It's not something I want happening to my best friend, but

I can no more stop *him* in his mission than he could *me* in mine. Now please, tell me where you met him."

"There is much to tell. How much do you want to know?"

"Everything."

Ipsah bit her lip. "The Gueritac captured me and my neighbors in our village...Ballant. There is nothing left."

"Where does Faelan come in?"

"Three days. An elfin village was plundered. He was among them. He was put in the irons behind mine."

"Is he okay now? Where is he? How did you get free?"

"He is fine, but I know not where he is. He said he was going with the dark-winged creature, but I did not stay long enough to see where he went."

"But how did you get free? Is he safe now?"

"We were freed by Dark Angel, and unlocked by the dark-winged creature. Whether she is Dark Angel or Faelan is safe, I do not know. I wish I did."

"Shhh...There is no need to cry. I can find out if he's okay right now. Here, do you see this?"

Ipsah looked at what the fairy held—a ring with the same flower as Faelan had imprinted upon her palm. "Yes. It is beautiful."

"Well, I can contact him with this. Here." She held out a glowing hand. "You can speak to him too."

***

The moon had made three-quarters of its journey across the sky and the fire had fizzled to only a dozen orange coals. Yet Faelan remained awake, staring at the halfling with fascination surpassing exhaustion.

In sleep her face did not twist into a scowl, but remained in a serene resting position. The softer expression caused the scars to be forgotten. Her lips had a lovely black curve and her eyes, though closed, reminded one of how lovely they were when open. She was exquisite.

He beat his hands against his chest. He had no shirt and the cooler the night got, the less comfortable he became. But she must also be cold. He went to the tent to retrieve two blankets and brought them out, placing one over Angel's sleeping form and wrapping the other gently around his shoulders.

He continued to look upon Angel's motionless shape with strange intensity. He had heard of halflings before. They were rare creatures—at least, they were in the places he'd been. Angel was the first halfling he had ever seen. He had not expected them to be so pretty.

"*Faelan.*"

Kaiya's voice. His sight found his hand, the ring on his finger shining the colors of the trillium flower. He set the ring on the ground and two fairies appeared in the form of shifting rainbow-shaded light.

"*Faelan!*" One said, rushing forward and throwing her arms around him. He felt only a warm breeze as she fell through him.

Kaiya laughed. "*Ipsah, you're not solid. You can't touch him.*"

"That might be a good thing." Faelan said as he turned to offer Ipsah his hand, though he knew she could not use it. "My back hurts much worse than it did earlier. A hug is not going to help it much."

"*Why does it hurt?*" Kaiya said, her shadow of light coming closer. "*Is that a welt on your neck?*"

Ipsah sobbed. "*I am sorry. I am so, so sorry.*"

"Hush, Ipsah." He said, letting his hand hover over her untouchable cheek. "You need not apologize. You did nothing to hurt me."

"*Faelan, would you please explain why your back hurts?*"

He glanced at Kaiya. She would not drop the subject. She would question until she got the answer she desired. His fists curled into balls, he took a breath, and he let the blanket fall from his shoulders.

She gasped.

He expected she would. He couldn't see his own back, but he had seen the backs of others who had been lashed. Not only did welts rise upon the skin, but sometimes bits of skin were torn away. No matter how gentle or heavy the beating, it always—*always*—had an ugly result.

"*What happened? Are you okay? Who…*"

"Kaiya please, don't worry about it. I'm fine. I have seen others with lashings ten times this bad."

"*Where did you get it?*"

He sighed. "When I was a prisoner of the Gueritac."

"*Why did you get it?*"

"*Because he carried me.*" Ipsah choked.

"*Why—*"

"She tripped, Kaiya. She was weak. Could we please not talk of this anymore?"

She sighed. "*Very well. But do tell me—who is she?*"

His eyes followed the direction of her glowing finger. "Her name is Angel. Don't worry about her. She likes me well enough, but she would probably like me less if she knew I had you here."

"*Why?*"

"She doesn't like faeries."

"*Fascinating.*" Kaiya said, crouching to get a better look at the halfling. "*Tell me more about her.*"

"She's a warrior. Her voice, words, and actions back it up almost to the end."

"*Almost? What do you mean 'almost'?*"

20

"I have told you before how warriors are crude, irritable and stubborn. Well, she *is* irritable, and she *is* stubborn—but only to a point. She likes harmony and her manner of speaking and acting are curled with tenderness. She is not a thorough warrior. Something has kept her civilized."

Kaiya looked up at him, the green light of her eyes shadowed for a moment with the gold of circulating colors. "*She has family.*"

"And that family is likely the person she wished to stay up for."

Kaiya sighed. "*I know what will come next. We are going to go with her, after a halfling who looks a lot like her. But there was a scene…I dare not say right now. Is there another reason you wished me to contact you?*"

"I need you to contact Ytoran and have him come to a town called Toriq. She told me it is the nearest village."

"*Alright. I'll contact him, but there's a different place I am going to send him.*"

"Where?"

"*You'll be there when he gets there, so you don't need to know.*"

"What are you up to? Come, Kaiya, you can tell me."

"*Sorry Faelan.*" She said with a twinkle in her eye. "*If I told you everything I would never be able to surprise you.*"

He smiled. "I used to say that to a little violet-wing. Is this some sort of revenge?"

"*Only if you let it be.*" She laughed. Then she took Ipsah's hand and waved a farewell. "*I'll see you soon.*"

The shimmering figures faded into darkness. They left behind no trace of their presence—they had not been present to leave a trace behind. He braided the ring back into his hair and wrapped the blanket about his shoulders, trapping the warmth of his body against the cold. As much as he now anticipated seeing Kaiya, he had to wonder if Angel would put up with her at all.

\*\*\*

Kaiya wiped the tears from Ipsah's eyes. "Calm down. He's safe. Isn't that what you wanted to know in the first place?"

She nodded, but continued to weep. "Wh-what if he gets an infection? Can you use your magic to cure him?"

She brushed another tear from the fairy's cheek. "No. I can't. Not right now anyways. My magic is faith-based and if I don't have enough faith I can't use my magic for it. You see this leg?" She pulled up the leg of her pants, revealing the jagged scars covering a majority of her calf. "It doesn't work the same way it used to. I limp everywhere. I can't fix it because I don't think it's in God's plan for it to be whole again. You see, I have this scar because I faced Isana and *lost* before I faced Isana and *won*. Our scars remind us of who we are—our failures and triumphs, our victories and defeats. We're all partial people. And, who knows, maybe Faelan will be better off for those scars."

Ipsah looked up, blue eyes glimmering. "Do you think he will be better off?"

Kaiya smiled. "Yes. God will work it out for the better. You'll see."

# Chapter Four

The remaining Gueritac set up camp as the sun kissed the eastern horizon. Some brought out cauldrons and lit fires, anxious to feed on the grains bought by blood, sweat and tears others shed. Others bandaged or tended wounds, and yet others stood guard against outside attacks.

Those not concerned with necessities drank whatever ale or wine they had procured from the last obliging town and lolled about in the sluggish fashion they found most enjoyable. They had none else to do because Shodak, the leader himself, stood guard over the sole remaining captive.

She sat bound with her head and back straight, glad for her thick black clothing. The chill of autumn would have bit through anything else. She, like the elf who held the fairy in his arms, refused to be broken, a holy fire glowing in her eye as she pretended compliance to Shodak's commands.

He, the Gueritac leader, stood over her with such blackness in his soul that it spilled from his dark eyes and stained warm colors a darker shade. The ugliness of his scowl abolished any handsome feature and though his shoulders were broad his face was too, and greed was the only thing that gave light to his countenance.

"I will ask you again." He growled, leveling his face with hers. "Where is your companion?"

"What companion do you speak of?"

The palm of his hand struck her cheek. "You *will* give me a straight answer! My blade drew blood but you are not bleeding. You have a companion as ugly as yourself, and only *you* know where to find her."

"At present I have no companion besides you."

His palm met her cheek again, bruising it a shade of black. "You know who I speak of. Tell me where she is, and I might spare your life."

She glared at him but saw he would snap if she did not give a closer answer. With a flick of her hair she answered. "I know not where she is. Dark Angel cannot be found. She finds you."

His palm hit her cheek a third time, the hardest yet. "She is not a ghost. She *can* be found and you know where to find her."

"I tell you I do not." She said, turning her head to expose the opposite cheek. "She could be anywhere from the sunrise coast to the end of the sunset map, from the southern desert to the northern snows. Do not ask me, a prisoner, to locate a leaf in the forest where I am not."

"I am not dealing with leaves." He growled. "I am dealing with something far more predictable. If you will not take me to her, she will come to me—and when I have defeated her there will be no reason for me to spare *you.*"

"Do not think your words can fool me," she said. "I know you will have no reason to release me if I help you. I have more chance of living and of being freed if I tell you nothing."

Several cuss words escaped his mouth, each meant to injure her to the very soul. But the foul language only fueled the fire in her heart and kept her hope alive. Nothing he said would break her spirit. Her heart could not be crushed.

***

Nocturnal creatures took refuge in their burrows as sunlight warmed the ground. A few birds began spouting melodious tunes to welcome the returning sun. A halfling stirred, her mind making a faint registration of a warm fire nearby and pain burning in her shoulder before falling back into a pleasant state of unconsciousness.

A curious-looking creature landed on the ground beside the halfling. Brown, birdlike wings folded down to the creature's half-human back, clicking sounds accompanying every movement. She walked on four scrawny limbs and poked the halfling with a brown, claw-like hand.

The halfling mumbled and sat up, still in lethargic in her consciousness. Then her mind was startled into vigilance and she scanned the clearing before fixing her attention on the nearest conscious creature. "Sil, has Mercy returned? Where is she?"

The wood nymph shook her head. "She was captured by the Gueritac last night."

"Captured? Where? You must take me to her."

"No." Sil said. "They are waiting for you. The leader, Shodak, knows there are two of you."

She closed her eyes. Mercy, captured? And the leader expected her to show up at any moment! This had never happened before —could not *be* happening! But Mercy was not there. That had never happened either. It distressed her beyond measure.

"So there is no way to get her back?" She asked. "I have lost her forever?"

"Maybe not." The nymph said. "What do you know of this healer?"

She looked at the sleeping healer, scabs and bruises fringing the dark blanket he had draped about his shoulders. He had been lashed. She had not noticed that the night before. Nor had she noticed, in the dark, the kind lines on his face and the way he kept his black hair in a long braid down his back. Darkness and fatigue, unfortunately, had robbed from her the pleasure of seeing the elf clearly.

"I know him to be a skillful healer and a good elf. What else am I supposed to know?"

"Last night I saw him speaking to apparitions after you had fallen asleep. They were beings made of light who stood before him and spoke to him as if physically in his presence. He called one Kaiya. Do you know the significance of that?"

"No."

"She is the queen of Criseyde! Perhaps you could convince her to give you help in retrieving Mercy."

"She is a fairy. She will not care to help me. I do not care to have her help me."

"She is your only hope. Do not be stubborn."

"Have you forgotten how cruel the faeries were? Do you think I should forgive them simply because they *might* be able to help me? I think not."

"I did not say to forgive them—only that you should consider asking them for help. At the very least they can begin to repay what they took away."

"They can never repay what they owe. I will *never* ask a faerie for help."

"Have it your way, then." The nymph said, raising her head in indignation. "I will see you when you choose to be reasonable."

With that, the nymph scampered to the nearest tree, climbing with the ease of a squirrel to the upper branches and disappearing in their leafless limbs. Angel watched with hardness in her expression, but her mind did not depart from Sil's words.

To ask help of this elf and of his friends was not possible—not with the amount she owed him. And he, a handsome young elf, a friend of faeries! It could hardly be fathomed.

But his kindness to the pink wing had not come from hatred toward them. Even Angel had to admit there was nothing unworthy in the fairy. The elf was simply rewarding weakness with strength, pain with healing, cruelty with kindness.

Did his kind treatment toward faeries make a difference? In his lifetime, how many faeries' prejudice had he rendered negligible with a kind action?

She picked up the medicine bag and rummaged through the contents. She had one herb in mind and she would settle for none other. She pushed aside healing plants of every kind until she found the desired herb—jipanti weed.

She emptied the pouch into a clean wooden bowl and poured water over them until she managed to grind out a thin paste. She took the corners of the healer's blanket and gently uncovered his torso.

She had seen worse. She had. It was common for Gueritac victims, especially elves, to endure beatings twice as brutal as the one evidenced on the healer's back. But she had never been their healer. She had never used her knowledge and abilities to heal the wounds of freed captives. It hurt to kneel over this elf, holding a salve for the injuries wrongly inflicted upon him. She could hardly bear it.

***

Warmth covered Faelan's back, calming every painful stripe he *had* and *still* felt. He pressed his eyelids down, trying to convince them to continue sleeping, to satisfy his desire for rest. But the sun would not be blocked out. He finally opened his eyes and sat up, pulling the blanket close to keep out the cold air.

"It is about time you woke up."

Angel sat several feet to his left, her arms crossed and tone annoyed. She pointed to a lump of fabric near the fire. "Those are for you. They are darker than your trousers, but they are all I have available. Put them on. The fire has warmed them suitably."

He took the clothing and let the blanket fall, feeling oddly subconscious about the bareness of his torso. It had seemed like nothing in the dark, and even less when he had a punisher breathing down his neck. But under Angel's gaze, his bare back embarrassed him. Did she have to stare at him so?

"Thank you."He said.

"It is not your task to thank me." She replied, her features impossibly cold. "It is the least I can do to repay your kindness."

"What kindness?"

She stared at him, but said nothing.

"Has the person you were waiting for shown up yet?"

A flash darted through Angel's eyes. "No."

"But you know where she is."

She glared. "Captured by the Gueritac. In saving you and your fellow captives, I lost a companion."

"I can help you get her back."

She glared at him. "I cannot ask that of you."

"You are not asking it, nor am I offering it. I am insisting on it, as is a friend of mine. She is to meet us en route."

"What sort of 'friend' do you speak of?"

"Queen Kaiya. She has been a friend of my tribe and of mine for a long time."

"She is a faerie?" The warrior girl growled.

"Yes." Faelan said.

She scowled. "No faerie will help me."

"You do not need to like her, though I know few who do not. You need only let her aid you in retrieving your sister."

This provoked a reaction.

"I said *nothing* of her being my *sister*! I said only she was a *companion*. Where could you get such an idea?"

"I saw it in your eyes."

"How? How could you see it in my eyes? The only way you could do that is to be a—" She stopped, her anger dimming. "You are a padparadscha?"

He bowed. "Since the age of twelve."

"And what else do you see?"

He looked at her pale gray eyes and dug deep into their seemingly indifferent emotions. "You are afraid of losing your sister. You are feeling contempt and surprise, but you like me well enough to overlook the contempt."

She glared. "You flatter yourself."

"I never say anything if it is not the truth."

Her face now held nothing but annoyance. "I do not enjoy being seen through so easily."

"Most folks don't. Still, you can't refuse my help, or the help of my friends. Your eyes tell me that too."

A deep growl came from her throat. "I *can* refuse. I *will* refuse. I will not have a fairy as a friend!"

The halfling jumped upon her horse and kicked it into a gallop before Faelan could speak any other objection.

Faelan's temper, however, cannot be underestimated. Her stubborn refusal of help coupled with her apparent desire of being killed propelled him forward. His feet slammed through and over rotten logs as his rage-smeared run drove him closer to her and her horse. A pair of hands grabbed him and tossed him into the air.

He knew the maneuver. He needed no warning to complete it. Even the surprise of the moment couldn't cause him to make a mistake. From the air he fell and he landed squarely on a centaur's back.

"Nice to see you Ytoran." Faelan said.

"From the look of your feet I got here just in time."

"Never mind my feet." He said. "Stop her. She'll kill herself if she keeps this up."

"I am under orders to keep up to her, not to stop her. Sorry."

Faelan groaned. "What does Kaiya have against keeping Angel alive?"

"I do not think she has anything against it. Have faith in her orders for now, Faelan. She may have a good reason."

Those words tamped out the sparks of anger. Kaiya wasn't the sort of queen who gave orders because she had the power to. Every order she gave was done strictly under orders from a Higher Source.

With the adrenaline no longer numbing him, Faelan realized what Ytoran meant by 'the looks of his feet.' His temper had propelled him barefoot through every sharp stick, stone and splinter. The pain of those things had not been sensed when he concentrated on reaching his goal, but now he had no reason to concentrate.

From the pain in his feet, he knew they had several sticks and splinters in them, some of which would have to be removed in following days when white bubbles formed around them and made them easier to extract. If he'd kept his head he would have spared himself several days of discomfort.

He had no bandages or salves to wrap his feet with, so he pulled out the sticks and rocks and let them be. He could work on them later. For now he returned his attention to Angel.

She did not appreciate Faelan following her, much less that he had little trouble doing so. She knew centaurs could run far faster than horses. But each time she turned and scowled at them, he saw a spark of curiosity in her eye. She wanted to know why he followed her. She wanted to know how he'd gotten a centaur. But most of all, she wanted to know why he refused to give up on her.

He had a reason for the last question. He saw it in her eyes.

# Chapter Five

In all her days, Angel had not seen such a stubborn elf. Never. No elf had *insisted* on helping her. No elf had run a half-mile to aid her. And no elf she knew could call a centaur at will.

No elf, excepting Healer Faelan.

She kicked Dorsey harder, but she knew it would be no use. Centaurs could run five times faster and longer than a horse—faster and longer if they had reason to. She had no hope of outrunning them. She had no choice but to accept his help. She almost did not mind. For the first time, a creature outside her family chose to care about her.

When elves or faeries looked upon her, they only saw what separated her from them. Black skin, black wings, pointy ears and pale gray eyes served to divide her from one or both species. Neither species treated her as a comrade, friend, or fellow creature. Because of this she had learned to discourage them from the start. Life was less painful when she expected no goodness and they expected the same.

The healer was different. His goodness made him charming, and his charm made her want to be good. He seemed to want her nearer, to touch her and hold her tight—No. He did not want that of her. She wanted it of him. If she asked him to hold her as he had the pink-wing, his goodness would give it to her. She had no doubt of that. But because of his goodness, she dared not ask.

In the bat of an eyelash the throbbing in her shoulder became a volcanic eruption. A fae dragged her off Dorsey's back and onto the ground. She almost screamed but a hand clamped tight over her mouth and pinned her arms and wings to her body.

"Let's take 'em back to the camp."

"Ya' think we'll get some coin off that townsman we spotted earlier?"

"He's got fancy enough clothes. If nothin' else we'll strip him of that and tie him with these two."

It took until this moment for Angel to realize her situation. No, these creatures were not Gueritac. They were thieves. They sold goods and fellow-creatures to the Gueritac for paltry prices. And she was their captive.

The thief tossed her down, her back slamming into a tree trunk, and he yanked her arms backward. She yelped, but had not the energy to scream. It would have done her no good if she had.

The pain settled to a steady burn and she realized her wrists had been bound to another's. They were rough wrists, like scabs and scratches covered the skin. Like they had been held in the Gueritac's rusty shackles.

She struggled for breath and observed the area. A single guard watched them as he stirred gruel over the fire. Would he object if she spoke? She did not fear the lash. As intense as pain could be, she would rather bear it than leave Faelan in silence. She would ignore the pain breathing caused. She would speak.

"Healer Faelan."

"Angel? Are you okay?"

"I am fine, Healer Faelan." She gasped, unable to recover the strength of her first few words. "Are you okay?"

"Yes."

"Good." She said, trying to draw in more breath. "Good."

"I'm sorry about this."

He should not be sorry! She knew the woods and should have realized thieves would lurk about wherever prey might tread. She should have kept her weapon drawn and her eye upon the road ahead. He was not at fault.

She tried to say this. She took in a breath and tried to spew the words like Mercy might have. But the breath caused her shoulder, in its painful position, to flare into suffocating pain, and only a deep groan escaped her.

"Angel, are you okay?"

She nodded, but he could not see it. She knew this. But what else could she do? The pain in her shoulder pulled the breath from her lungs, and the grief of Faelan's returned fate pained her. It pained her more than words could describe, had she been willing to speak such words.

"You're not okay." He said. His hand moved gripping at her limp hand. "I cannot twist far enough. Take my hand, Angel."

This time she managed a reply. "Why?"

"I can help you. Trust me."

She gasped for a breath, the strangulation of pain and position making this almost impossible. "I trust no one."

"You can trust me."

She could not accept more help from him. She could not. But with all her strength drained by pain—a type of drain she had not felt for years—she had little choice.

All the burning in Criseyde seemed concentrated on her shoulder as she turned her hand. Faelan's hand grasped hers, and she curled her fingers around it. She felt a jerk, heard him wince, and warmth stretch up her arm, covering her injured shoulder.

The warmth ebbed away and left a lesser pain in its place. The hand she gripped loosened, but she held fast, and Faelan wrapped his tighter again. She took a deep breath, appreciating the ability to breathe.

"Is that better, Angel?"

"Yes, Healer Faelan." She replied. "How did you do that?"

"I used the magic from...I cannot say what it is."

In other words it was valuable, likely a piece of jewelry he had hidden from view. "Can you use the magic to free us?"

"No."

"Why? Does it only heal and not do any other task?"

"It can do many tasks, but I can only use it if the task is God's will."

She turned her head his direction, though she would not be able to see any more than his shoulder. "And being free is not the will of God?"

"Not right now. Kaiya is coming for us, so freeing us would have done what would have been done anyways. However, it will do no good if you're incapacitated when she gets here."

"And how do you know your faerie friend is coming?"

"The...the magic lets me speak to her over distances—"

"That is not possible."

"Oh, but it is!" He said, squeezing her hand tighter. "Her magic is almost unlimited. She's a violet wing, and she has the combined magic of all the faeries who ever lived to draw from."

She scowled. "That is not possible either."

"Angel, please believe me. I speak only the truth—I told you that—and I *know* Kaiya is coming for us. When I spoke to her, she mentioned she'd had a dream, but she was reluctant to give me any details. This must be the reason."

Angel could say nothing to this. As foolish as it sounded, they had little else to hope for. And Mercy could not be saved while they remained captives themselves. But not to speak at all could cause a collapse within. She had never been in this position. She had never been the captive. She had spent her life *releasing* captives—and not all of them at that. How those faeries must have felt!

"Angel, are you okay?"

She took a breath and tried to wipe the tear from her eyelashes. "Yes, Healer Faelan. Please, tell me the appearance of your magic. What does it look like?"

"It is lovely—sparkling and gemlike. But they are not real gems. Have you ever seen a painted trillium?"

"I do not know that name. What is it?"

"It is a flower with three petals, three sepals and three leaves. The petals are very unique in that they are white and have red veins reminiscent of bloodstains. It is Kaiya's favorite flower."

"I believe I know the flower. And this holds some of Kaiya's magic?"

"Yes. It doesn't hold very much, but it was enough to make you more comfortable."

"How does it hold the magic? The magic cannot be ingrained in the stone."

"No, there is no stone to it. She actually cut her hand and let blood drip out, capturing it with magic and molding her blood and the magic into the shape of the petals. She made the sepals with my blood, for I made an identical cut on my hand. Then she captured sunlight and encased it in a deep yellow heliodor."

"You describe the making, but how does it hold the magic?"

"Kaiya's blood. Magic is made in the wings of a faerie, but it is stored in the blood. By putting her blood in the trinket and placing my blood beside it, she gave me the power to use what little magic can be stored in the ring."

"Ring?"

The heart within Angel nearly ceased beating. Had the fae been listening? Would he steal Faelan's precious trinket? She leaned her head against the tree and squeezed Faelan's hand. He squeezed it back.

"I said," Faelan growled "My back stings. I was whipped recently and the bark of the tree is aggravating the pain."

"Aw, shut up then." The fae snarled. "You'll give me a headache."

Angel had no reason to speak again. To drown in failure would be enough. *She* had been the cause of their capture. Her inability to win this fight had left Mercy in the Gueritac's hands and would lead her to the same fate.

Or might the fairy come through?

If only she could control her magic better! If she could direct her magic toward the rope, she could free them easily. But the sparks she could create would spew everywhere and burn everything in their vicinity—the wrists of the captives especially. She would not further injure the healer's wrists by her magic gone amiss. But the gentleness of his one hand made her long to hold the other. She moved her other hand, trying to wrap her fingers around Faelan's. He seemed to sense this and took it, holding her hand tight. Oddly, it made their position far more comfortable.

"It is okay, Angel." He said. "I know how you feel right now. You don't need to speak."

"You are much like Mercy." Angel whispered.

"How so?"

"Mercy never let me down. She said things to comfort me whether she meant them or not. She never made me speak. You would like her, I believe."

"You are right on two of three counts. I will never let you down if I can help it, and I will never make you speak if you do not wish to; but I mean what I say. I feel your failure and defeat, your pain and bitterness. I feel it for my own reasons, but I still feel it."

"Why? Why do you feel these horrible things? You have faith in Kaiya and your God. Why should you be so unhappy?"

He sighed and squeezed her hands. "You would not understand, lovely Angel. I must bear my cross alone."

She did not pursue the subject. She changed the conversation and kept her hands entangled with Faelan's. Of his goodness, she knew she could ask this much. She only wished it did not indebt her so much more.

***

A sound brushed Faelan's ear. Silence followed and the darkness closed back in. He squeezed Angel's hand.

She growled. "I am awake. You need not bruise me."

"Listen."

"To what? There are only a few crickets."

"Listen harder."

The sound started again, soft as an owl's wing-beat. It could almost be mistaken as Angel's crickets or the hoots of an owl. But Faelan knew the voice and he joined the song.

Then it quit. He could hear only the crickets. But he kept singing. If she desired him to sing he would continue until she said otherwise.

"Keep singing."

Kaiya! A lump rose in his throat and he almost stopped singing, but he forced the song through the constricted passage. Angel whispered "He was right."

"Faelan is often right." Kaiya said. "Where are your hands? I can't see well in this light. Ah, good. Keep your fingers out of the way. There. Help me with the other wrists now."

He felt her sawing at the ropes, followed by the same sweet release Angel had given him by unlocking his shackles. Angel's hand did not immediately release his, but when it did he pulled Angel into an embrace.

He did not expect what he felt. He had expected her to stiffen and push him away. Perhaps he should have taken the way she'd held his hand as a sign of what would happen. But how could he have seen, from her behavior and hostility, that she would wrap her arms around him with more speed than he did her.

Her arms held him with tenderness and ease, seeming conscious of his stripes and taking care not to hurt him. The way her fingertips pressed into his shoulder and her face buried itself in his chest kept him still and left him wondering if she would allow him to plant a kiss upon her cheek. With all her sharp words and angry expressions, he had never expected she could be so tender.

But he *had* to release her. Kaiya's curiosity would soon be stirred and would lead to questions. Questions would detract from rescuing Mercy. Angel needed Mercy more than she needed his arms.

He released Angel and turned to the fairy queen, awaiting her instructions. He did not need to wait long.

"Okay." Kaiya said, clapping her hands together. "Here's what we are going to do...don't stop singing, Faelan. It's our cover. It keeps them from knowing I'm here."

He started singing again and listened as best he could to what Kaiya said. She had already released Ytoran and he had joined the rest of their group. He and Angel, on the other hand, would join Kaiya in a bit of non-violent justice.

He could tell Angel liked Kaiya's plan. Not only did her eyes show interest and agreement, but they showed very little dislike. The opportunity arose, after the plan was discussed, for Kaiya to ask whether Angel had any magical powers and what their maximum strength was, she answered readily that halflings could not make magic as quickly as faeries and if she were to use all of her magic—enough to save a life or destroy it—she would never be able to use magic again.

"But," Angel said "I can use little bits at a time. I can create sparks enough to light a fire and mend clothes without using a needle—certain aspects, however, are poorly controlled and I have not the resources to improve them."

Kaiya nodded, her eyes twinkling. "I think you can have quite a lot of fun tomorrow. You must rest now, and we will carry through tomorrow."

# Chapter Six

The fairy queen had quickly earned Angel's favor. All her new companions had fire in their eyes, but Kaiya had something of an intelligence, curiosity and joy. Angel could not dislike a creature like her.

Angel harbored no dislike for any of the other creatures, however. Ranger, Kaiya's husband, had goodness in his features and conversed with Faelan like he would a friend. Angel had offered Ipsah an apology for the pain she caused and the pink-wing had accepted it happily. Knowing Angel would forever unlock all innocent creatures from the Gueritac's grip seemed to give Ipsah a glow of pride. These three faeries, Angel concluded, were actually pleasant, unprejudiced creatures. She would like to spend time around them.

A robin's song trilled through the forest. Kaiya and Faelan both raised their heads.

"Did I hear what I think I heard?" Kaiya asked.

"Yes." Faelan said, standing. "A robin's call. They should have all flown south."

"Could it be another of the thieves?"

The direction of this conversation alarmed Angel. "No. This is all of them." She said, motioning to the half-dozen fae they had tied to trees. "It is likely a mocking bird or a jay. I will investigate for you."

Before either Kaiya or Faelan had a moment to protest she tied a scabbard and sword about her waist and fled to the woods.

"Sil." She called. "Where are you? Sil?"

A clicking sound like the snapping of twigs and the rush of flapping wings announced Sil's arrival. "You changed your mind."

"I had no choice. I called for you yesterday but you did not come to my aid. Faelan's faerie friends did."

Sil scowled. "Now they have rescued you from your most feared fate you do not mind them? I thought they could never repay their debt to you."

"They cannot. But..."

"But they are not the sort of faeries who owe you a debt." Sil said. "They are like Mercy and Edan."

Angel would not agree with this. She could not disagree with it either. Instead she said, "Why did you not come? Or even had you *warned* me of the thieves I would not have been taken captive. Why did you not help me?"

"When Healer Faelan spoke to Queen Kaiya she mentioned a dream she did not wish to disclose completely. Perhaps that was the dream, or perhaps it was not. In either case I had enough on my hands trying to keep my bird friends from eating a villager's sunflower seeds."

"Angel!"

Sil looked toward the sound. "It appears your elf friend is calling you. I will return later and give you Shodak's location."

The nymph took wing and disappeared among the treetops. Angel turned and found Faelan only a few feet away.

"It was a mockingbird."

He gripped her arm before she could pass him by. "You are a fool."

She scowled. "What did you say?"

"You heard me, Angel." He said, his grip tightening. "You are a fool. You leave the camp without a companion and seek out a sound which is as out of place as a snowflake in midsummer. With your experience I expected you to have more caution."

"Gueritac move only in the darker hours. They will not be out at this time of day."

"What about the thieves? It was precisely this time of day when they attacked."

She glared at him only to find his glare upon her.

"We are returning to the camp. You may be used to being alone, but you need to play by our rules now. The Gueritac already know yours."

She scowled but bowed her head. "Very well."

Protest did not occur to her. Recent events proved his words to be correct. What other explanation could be rendered? Shodak's partial victory shattered her certainty. Only thorough knowledge of her tactics could have produced such a result.

Predictable. The continual reuse of a dozen procedures had led to Dark Angel's movements becoming predictable. But Angel had not the ability to create such maneuvers, nor did Mercy. They owed all they had to their brother.

The clearing returned to her vision. Kaiya remained around the fire with a kettle to heat the thieves' breakfast. Faelan had informed Kaiya of the food which they had prepared for supper and she had copied it precisely—but she had added a few ingredients. Now the smell awoke the senses and demanded the taste buds take notice. Angel was surprised the aroma alone had not woken the thieves.

The thieves' position seemed most uncomfortable. Tied in the same fashion as she and Faelan had been, Angel wondered how they could *sleep* in the same position which rendered her and Faelan unable to rest at all. Perhaps Kaiya had done too good a job in magically promoting their slumber. Perhaps they never would awaken.

Kaiya dished out the food in generous amounts and handed the bowls to Ranger, Angel and Faelan. Angel and the rest of her conscious companions had eaten their share of this breakfast earlier—these bowls were destined for the sleeping thieves.

They did not deserve something so good.

She kicked the thigh of a particularly filthy thief and shouted for him to awaken. He did so with a snort and a shout. The rest of the thieves followed this up with a terrible uproar. None of them had gone to sleep bound, yet they woke to the shock of being tangled in a snarl of well-tied ropes. How could this have happened?

"Shut up." Angel barked. "Or I will stuff your mouths with shoes instead of breakfast fare."

This quieted them, as the smell captured their stomachs and made them long for the food they were offered. She placed the bowl in the fae's lap, scowled, and untied one hand so they could eat. Then she returned to Kaiya for a second bowl.

"In case you're wondering," Kaiya said. "My crew and I tied you up like that last night. I don't take kindly to anyone who wrongfully deprives creatures of their possessions and freedoms."

General discomfort spread among the thieves. A few seemed to have lost their appetite. Angel did not care. She delivered the second bowl and took her place beside Faelan, sharpening her sword with a hard whet stone.

The appearance of such an angry, battle-scarred creature as Angel sharpening a sword was something frightful. She had been *their* captive the day before. This made her even more frightful. Pleas for mercy began spouting forth and the thieves pointed out their shabby dress compared to the warm, well-made clothes which their captors wore.

"Shut up." Angel shouted, brandishing her sharpened sword in their direction. "You had as much chance to gain good clothes such as these by working as farmers, soldiers and blacksmiths. Why should we show you mercy when you pilfer the things we work hard to acquire?"

"Moreover," Kaiya added, "I have full authority to do with you as I wish."

"What are you?" One snorted. "The queen?"

"Actually," Angel said, scraping the whet stone particularly hard against the blade "She is."

The fae's dirty hands trembled and the breakfast bowl spilled some of its contents. When he spoke again his voice could hardly be heard. "You are the queen?"

"I am. This," She motioned to Ranger, "Is King Charranger. And these three," waving toward Angel, Faelan and Ytoran "Are my friends. The elf and the centaur, Faelan and Ytoran, are missionaries—they did not come to fight but to spread God's word. Angel, the halfling, is a warrior. She is on her way to free her sister from a Gueritac band. Your intent was to sell them or, if you had known of my friendship, you would have requested ransom. Tell me, then, whose cause is nobler?"

This might have caused an uproar of self-pity had not Angel's sword been in full view and the whet stone making an unnerving sound against its blade. A different fae appeared to be gathering his courage to say something, but Angel sent a wisp of magic in his direction, sewing his shirt collar tight against his throat and vaporizing all the nerve he possessed.

"Of course you are wondering what I will do with you." Kaiya said, taking the stone from Angel and giving her a leather strop to finish it on. "It is simple. What you were to do to my friends will be done to you."

The captives hung their heads and a few broke out in tears. Angel savored this sight. She had never seen such a fae broken.

"From what I hear," Kaiya continued "You will spend your days in hard labor, earning nothing but lashes for your back and enough food for survival. You won't own anything—not even yourselves. It's the same life you sent numerous others into. It sounds like a dream come true, doesn't it?"

"I do not agree with that punishment."

Faelan's words shocked the thieves into silence. For a time they could not decipher his meaning. Then those who had been sobbing showed hope of some small measure and those who had not began shedding tears in despair.

"What do you mean?" Kaiya asked. "Am I not severe enough upon them?"

"If they are repentant there need be no selling—or giving, as I know you would never accept blood money—there is only the need of finding folks who will take them under their wings and teach them honest trades."

"But what of the others they sold into slavery?" Angel growled. "They should atone for their past actions. Death is, perhaps, the best reward for them."

"Angel," Kaiya said "Faelan has a point. They may be of use, for that matter." She looked at the captives with a sparkle in her eye. "How are your acting skills?"

Angel had held onto her doubts for a time, but the plan had been worth a try. The thieves now would be instrumental in saving Mercy. Unfortunately, the thieves would be released afterward to tradesmen willing to apprentice ex-thieves.

Kaiya explained her plan to the thieves and, though some seemed concerned, most of them seemed willing to follow through. The thieves would remain bound, but they would not be treated with contempt.

Angel's only task in this plan had been to aid in intimidating the captives. The remainder of the plan placed her far outside the Gueritac's reach. Faelan, Ytoran, the royals and the black unicorn would be used. Even the thieves had a place in the plan. Only she and Faelan's pink-wing had been left out.

She understood the logic of the matter. She could be recognized by Shodak and the pink-wing could be recognized from her captivity. They could shatter the effectiveness of the plan by being included, so they were left out.

But she did not like it.

"What are you thinking about?"

Angel scowled at Faelan. "Your fairy's plan."

"She is not *my* fairy."

"She might as well be. I am not a padparadscha, but even an imbecile can see the way you drool and fawn over her."

"Enough! Tell me your thoughts about her plan."

"I do not like doing nothing. She has me in a lookout position and the pink-wing—"

"Ipsah."

"And *Ipsah*," she drawled "Is naught but a mouth to feed on the trip. I see not why she came at all but to fawn over you the same way you do over the queen."

"Angel!" He glanced toward the pink-wing, who slept not far away. "You should not say such things."

"Do I not speak the truth? Does *Ipsah* not lean on your words with excessive admiration? It is what you get for being her hero. What did Kaiya do to deserve such respect from you?"

He ran his hand over his hair and wound his braid around his fingers. "Who would not admire a girl as strong, wise and joyful as she? Kaiya is a paragon of goodness."

"Such a comment is a matter of opinion." Angel replied.

Faelan looked at her. "You do not see her generosity and goodness, her knowledge and her wisdom? Tell me, if you *do* see these things, what you see in her that isn't desirable."

"I can say nothing against her that you would believe."

He looked at her, a temper flaring in his eyes. But he tamped it down and discerning appeared before he said: "You are jealous of her. But why? What does she have that you don't?"

"That, Healer Faelan," she replied "You are not entitled to know. I suggest you return to your queen and fawn over her further."

"I have no reason to." He said. "She does not need my help."

"Nor do I, Healer Faelan. I suggest you seek out someone who does."

He might have replied to this, but the help came to him, as Ranger called him to aid in some task or other. He walked away with only a glance back.

"Yes." Angel whispered. "Go find someone else to help. You have helped me too much already."

# Chapter Seven

Ipsah's eyes could not stop roving as she observed her companions. Ranger walked with Kaiya's hand in his, his fingers sweetly entwined with hers. Puritan cantered ahead, his silver horn gleaming in the afternoon sun. Angel stood tall, walking with a confident air that defied the existence of her injuries. And then there was Faelan.

He limped and winced on occasion, talking to Angel of every subject imaginable. Had Ipsah had the strength, she would have kept up and listened to their words...but the courage and strength could not be summoned. Instead, she lagged behind.

"Ipsah." The centaur said. "You are limping. Ride on my back for a time."

"No thank you." She said. "We are resting you that you may carry us later. I do not want to tire you."

"I insist." He said. "Faelan carried you among the Gueritac for a reason. You are not up to walking many miles on feet such as yours."

She looked down at her feet, but no skin showed from them. Kaiya had equipped her with warm goat-skin boots before they left Idlerose. Faelan, on the other hand, wore naught but a spare pair of moccasins they had found at the thieves' camp.

"Faelan needs rest more than I." She said.

"No. Faelan is strong and stubborn, he will not ride when there are not enough horses and centaurs—and unicorns, in this case—for all his companions to ride upon. Your legs wobble with each step and Faelan will hold me accountable if you drop from exhaustion."

A pang of guilt propelled Ipsah onto Ytoran's back. It did not take her long to feel comfortable enough to ask for some of the centaur's knowledge.

"How long have you known Faelan?"

The centaur turned his head slightly. "Over three years. Why do you ask?"

She blushed and answered "I was just wondering."

Ytoran was silent for a time as his hooves clopped against the ground. When he did speak, he spoke in a low voice. "You love him."

"Am I wrong to love him?"

"Not as far as goodness is concerned. All the girls in his tribe wanted to wed him, but none of them could meet his standards after he met Kaiya. He will not marry a fairy, though. He is not attracted to them."

Ipsah shrank. "What was his kindness to me then? His goodness must branch from love...mustn't it?"

The centaur shook his head. "Not the sort of love you may think. He hates no one, wishes to help everyone, and sometimes singles out vulnerable people to show peculiar kindness to. It is in his nature. He cannot help it. The love you sensed is what he calls 'the love of God's children.' It is the same love he would show to anyone else in your situation."

Ipsah did not offer a reply. She only pointed to Kaiya and asked another question. "She is the fairy Faelan sees as his model? What is she like?"

"She is strong, courageous and knowledgeable. I don't think she has been timid since the time she first met Faelan—she tried to kill him, you know."

Ipsah gasped, but the centaur continued his description. "She's an excellent fighter. She's gone into battle against fae three and four times her size and come out victorious. She refuses to be passive and she's always working toward being the protector of her people. If she had loved him as much as he did her, and had she been an elf, she would have been his choice."

*** 

The reasons for not traveling at night were as numerous as the stars in the sky, the largest being the propensity for stumbling over rocks, branches and through streams. Who in their right mind would walk when they could not see the path they are treading upon?

For that same reason it is a time when the Gueritac move. They could strip a town of its valuable inhabitants and disappear into the blackness before other towns can be alerted. Gueritac loved the dark.

But Shodak had a plan that did not require nighttime travel. He reveled before Mercy, telling her of his upcoming triumph, and detailing the techniques he would use to kill her and her sister. Mercy kept her countenance and refused to lose the fire in her eyes. She did not speak, but listened as words meant to burn and dishearten her only fueled her desire to break free. Finally, when the gleeful malevolence could grow no stronger, she opened her mouth.

"You will lose. You can kill me, you can kill Dark Angel, you can kill anyone else, but the only life that will be lost is your own. Upon your death, who will seek your face and cry for your pain? Who will mourn your loss? Not I, not Dark Angel, not even your followers will mourn over you. In the end victory is never in the hands of hatred."

Shodak growled, his malice no longer gleeful. "You still are not broken. You are a stubborn, foolish girl. Let's see how stubborn you are when—"

He had no chance to finish his sentence. A thunderous roar echoed through the camp and he ran to see the cause. She took a breath, thankful to be relieved of his presence, though it would not be more than a few moments.

Another fae entered, and she prepared to show him the same acidity shown to Shodak, but as he turned, she saw his face and she could hardly keep from shouting in joy. "Jas! I thought—we could not—where—"

He put a finger to his lip and she quieted, but as he untied the ropes, she could not help feeling overpowered and overjoyed. She could not help saying "I never stopped looking for you."

He smiled and kissed her, but he wasted no more time. "I heard of your capture, so a friend and I have come to break you out."

"How? And what was that sound? And what—"

"Shhh…" he said, as he finished untying her hands. "Tie my hands now. My friend and I have a plan. Hurry, my love, we have little time."

"But Shodak—he will kill you—"

His eyes shone pale gray as he clasped her hand. "Trust me, Mercy. You have to trust me."

# Chapter Eight

Stars twinkled in the sky and the moon gazed down with illuminated indifference. Nothing moved, nothing spoke. This was the time when Angel had always been at home. It was her only home.

From the time of her childhood she had lived the dark. Whether winter or summer, spring or fall, she adored hiding among the trees and observing the world of darkness. Even when there was nothing to see or do, she could be found sitting in blackness and soaking in the absence of light.

She could never explain it. Sometimes she thought it might be the color of her blood tainting her desires. Or perhaps being invisible spared her the cruel looks of her faerie neighbors. The likeliest reason, however, was the nature of the darkness itself.

Darkness held mystery. In darkness one feared what could not be deciphered and the imagination ran rampant, trying to fill nothing with something, whether or not it comforted the creator of the visions. The truth was skewed by the subconscious of the observer...and in some cases the truth was not skewed at all: it was revealed.

"Angel? What are you doing out here?"

She scowled at the healer's dark shape. "I am used to remaining awake for half the dark hours."

"I'm not, but the Gueritac and the thieves messed up my sleep cycle."

He sat down beside her and placed a hand on her shoulder. She winced.

"Oops." He said, "I forgot about that."

She heard him breathing. Mercy's breaths, during even the quietest nights, was never more than an infrequent reassurance of her existence. Faelan's deep breaths could be heard without trouble—a sign not only of his existence, but his presence and warmth. His breathing comforted her beautifully. She sighed. "I forget about it too."

He was quiet for a minute before he whispered "Are you thinking of your sister?"

"Some. There are many things to consider."

"Such as?"

She scowled. "There is no reason *you* need to know what is in *my* mind."

"Forgive me. I did not mean to offend you."

She had not expected such a brief answer. She leaned against his shoulder. His muscles tensed, relaxed, and he slowly placed his hand on her back. She breathed in. He smelled of dry blood and moss. Scents she knew well.

"You puzzle me, Angel."

"I do not see why."

"I'm not sure I do either." He said. "Your voice is so rough, your words stinging, and you looks scorching, but your touch is so tender I feel certain your body is disconnected from your mind."

She shrugged, but winced as the pressure area moved to her wound.

"Are you okay?"

"I am fine, Healer Faelan. You may stop asking me that now."

He sighed, his chest deflating with the movement. "I just worry about you. Most creatures would be in desperate pain."

"I get injured often." She said. "I cannot always feel pain."

"That can be a good thing."

She looked up at his face. "Is the flame being absent from your eyes also a good thing?"

"I don't know."

She touched his cheek. "Your face is handsome. It looks nicer when you have a flame in your eyes."

"And your face is pretty. You look much prettier when you smile."

She scowled at this remark. "I never have any reason to smile. Do you expect me to appear happy when I am plunging a sword into a faerie's heart?"

He sighed. "I have no reason to keep the flame burning in my eyes. Why should I keep the fire going when there is no one who needs it to burn?"

She could not offer a reply to these words. She simply maintained the warm, comfortable position she had established on his shoulder.

"I don't like fires." He said after a time. "They consume without creating. Even harnessing their heat for cooking destroys fuels that are, in some cases, older than you or I will ever be. What is the use of keeping a fire going for no reason but to have the flames?"

She said nothing. Truth could not be denied.

"Do you know, Angel, what it's like to see something you consider more valuable than gold, more valuable than life itself, consumed by flames?"

The distress in his voice was almost missed by that within her heart. He did not know of her circumstances. His words stemmed from his own pain.

"What is wrong, Healer Faelan?"

He shook his head. "Nothing, Angel. Do not trouble yourself."

Silence weighed like a brick upon Angel's stomach. She could see he would not open up unless she admitted a scourge of her own. But to admit such a thing! It would shred her heart like a burnt leaf. She could not!

But she owed Faelan much. It had taken her a full day to realize it, but she knew the reason she felt indebted to him. She had seen in him and the pink-wing what she had seen between her father and her mother. Though it was only a brief moment, she had been reminded of their sweetness and goodness. She could recall the life she once had. She wished she could have it again. He made her *feel*.

She owed him the truth.

"My heart is burnt by fire and can no longer function the way others do. I do not think it functions at all."

His arm wrapped around her less awkwardly than before. "Your heart can function. I have seen it."

"I do not want it to." She said. "It hurts to have a functioning heart. I prefer it to be burnt and useless."

He looked at her. "What caused this dark attitude?"

She looked up at his eyes and dug as deep as she could dig. "Do you know what it is like to see something you value more than gold, more than life itself, consumed by flames?"

He brushed hair from her cheek. "Our hearts are burned by fire and scorched by life's cruelties. You and I are just alike."

She was quiet for a while before she spoke again. "The fire in your eyes is not the kind which destroys things. Your fire creates and fans hope and goodness. I do not have such a fire in my eyes."

He sighed and drew her nearer. She savored it, for she knew she would not often have such a pleasure.

"You may think what I mourn is simple, for I know you lost much more." He paused and looked at her. "Promise you will not be angry."

She did as she was asked and looked at him with request of knowledge.

"It was," He said "Kaiya's Bible."

This *did* surprise her. It almost angered her. But she kept her head serenely placed on his shoulder. If the punishment for anger was the loss of Faelan's shoulder, it would be a most cruel penalty indeed.

"It was not an ordinary Bible." He said. "Queen Isana destroyed Kaiya's home and killed her parents. The Bible was one of the few things she salvaged from the ruins she returned to."

Now the idea of anger could not be found within her. Kaiya smiled and laughed so often, Angel had thought her incapable of sorrow. Now Kaiya seemed much like Angel. She wondered what had caused their paths to differ so widely.

"When Ranger left for two years," Faelan continued "his last gift was a trillium flower. She pressed it gently between the Bible's pages. When she was forced to flee, it was one of the few things she took with her. When I told her I was leaving on a mission trip, she placed that precious Bible and this ring in my hands and bid me farewell. There were so many stories connected to the Bible that when the Gueritac seized me, my only worry was for the book and the trillium pressed inside. When it touched the fire...I burst into flames too."

"The Gueritac," She whispered "destroy all the Bibles they encounter. They know little of its contents, but they know it does not speak kindly of their business."

She understood now. For only a few days his eyes had been dark and empty. For only a short time had he been truly hurt, damaged, in pain. And for a good cause.

"What did Kaiya do after her parents died?"

He looked down at her. "She leaned on my tribe for support. Her brother could not comfort her. Why do you ask?"

"Her story begins like mine. A fire consumed my house. Only my brother, my sister and I survived, and I killed the fae who set it. We were forced to flee when the village vied to separate my head from my neck the way I had several of their sons."

He pulled her closer, but this time she had decided she did not want comfort. She pushed away, but when she discovered a shock of cold air she returned to her warm position. In leaning on him she found not comfort, but silence. He did not say anything for a long while and when he did it came out in a soft, sweet voice she could not fight.

"If you believe you are the opposite of Kaiya, you are wrong. You are smart and sweet and wise beneath your callous and stubborn surface. If you stopped staring at the dark you would see the light."

"Then why do you not follow it? Why do you insist on mourning a book which, though it meant much, is worth far less than you are? If your God is real, He cannot be burned with a book. Mercy's God cannot. My God cannot."

For a time he was silent, then his lips pressed against her forehead, leaving a burning circle on her skin. He stood, and she could do naught but stand with him, trying to keep the warmth.

"You are right, Angel." He said. "I cannot lead creatures to the light without following it myself. Please forgive me." He turned to leave.

"Healer Faelan."

He turned back, sorrowful. "What do you want, Angel? What can I do for you?"

"I want to help you."

He shook his head. "The blind cannot lead the blind. You cannot lead me to a light you cannot see."

"Then let us find the light together."

The words were out before her mind gave her permission to speak them. He stood stunned and stared into her eyes. He tilted his head to the side and looked closer. "Do you believe in me as heartily as this?" He paused, the shape of his eyebrows softening into a sweet curve. "Do you want to find the same thing I must?"

Her shoulders sagged. "I do not know what I want."

"It's good you finally admit *that*. I've seen indecision in your eyes since we met. But I'm not sure I'm the right creature to help you."

She grasped his shoulder and turned him around, touching his back with her fingertips. He winced and tried to remove her hand, but she held him still. "This back," she said, fingering another one of the scabs "is a mark of commiseration. Your pain is mine. *I* cannot heal myself, *you* cannot heal yourself—but we *can* heal each other."

His eyes shone with adoration, like the expression he wore when he looked at Kaiya, but far deeper and sweeter. "I heal you, you heal me?"

"Yes." She said. "Exactly."

# Chapter Nine

Glimpses of a camp could be seen through the trees. It consisted mainly of covered wagons, tents and centaurs. Two dozen Gueritac sat around fires and leaned against wagons. But none of these things were of consequence. Only the prisoner interested them, and she was nowhere to be seen.

Faelan slid from Puritan's back. "She must be in one of the wagons."

"Yes." Angel said. "They keep their most valuable creatures in the wagons...especially if they have only one. I do not see why they value Mercy."

"That is simple." The black unicorn said, shaking its dark mane. "You tell us Shodak is expecting you. He must want revenge, and he considers that more valuable than any of his followers."

Angel glared at the unicorn, but the noble creature lifted its huge head and its silver eyes gleamed. "See, you are much like Shodak. Revenge is worth your life—and the lives of you siblings."

The unicorn galloped off with those words, as he was needed on the other side of the clearing. Angel hoped no one had paid attention to his words and ordered Ipsah to keep hold of Dorsey's reigns.

Like requesting someone to watch paint dry, holding Dorsey's reigns was a needless task. Dorsey did not wander far from Angel, and Angel rarely found occasion to tie it. Half the time she left it to roam, knowing Dorsey would always return.

Her hands gripped the branches of a nearby tree, and she readied to hoist herself up. A hand caught her injured shoulder. She winced, but she knew the meaning of the gesture before Faelan spoke a single word.

"Promise me." He said. "Promise you will stay out of sight unless I am in danger. You are too valuable a resource for this part of Criseyde to lose."

"Mercy is my sister." She scowled. "Shodak is my enemy. Only I have cause to fight this battle."

"Your pain is mine." He said. "Your battle is mine. Promise me, Angel, or I will not leave you."

"I...I promise."

He released her and she took a deep breath. Then, as she pulled herself into the bare limbs of the hardwood, Faelan disappeared into the brush.

She did not like this plan.

To place *her* life at risk would not have caused apprehension. She would have been thrilled with such a plan. But this plan put the healer's life at the tip of the Gueritac's sword. She did not like this plan at all.

Unfortunately, no better plan could be offered. Edan might have devised a far more cunning plan, but his whereabouts had not been known for over two years. She could not keep track of him once he reentered faerie society.

A group of faeries appeared on the outskirts of the Gueritac camp. She knew this as Faelan's cue to seek a safe entrance to the camp. It was *her* cue to make certain none of her friends were harmed.

The group consisted of seven fae and one fairy—six thieves, Ranger and Kaiya. All had wings painted pink, red or orange, for the Gueritac would not accept any stronger magic than that. A few of the thieves had not needed the paint. Ranger certainly had not.

Never had she met a Shape-shifter Clan. She had not known they existed until Faelan informed her of Ranger's clan. And the proof of these words made itself evident now.

With the little magic an orange wing had, Ranger had painted his face with the guise of a severe fae with a face so covered in scars none could doubt he was a thief or slave-trader. He rode upon Ytoran, as Puritan had been deemed too valuable, and two thieves walked behind him, pulling the 'captives' at the rear.

Kaiya was among the captives, a position Angel envied. Her wings had been painted a reddish shade of pink and her acting had been perfected by quizzing the healer, the pink-wing and Angel of the behavior captives exhibited. She looked as real with pink wings and a frightened expression as she did with violet wings and a smile the width of her wingspan.

But Angel could not watch the decoy. As the Gueritac took notice of the newcomers, Angel scanned the wagons for the object of her protection.

Creeping behind a covered wagon was Faelan, searching for an entrance to the wagons. She edged her way further up the tree trunk. She would not let them within ten feet of an elf like Faelan.

Faelan, the faerie-loving healer, was worth much to her. As they had stared at the stars, breathing in autumn and each other's breath, she had felt a sweet blush of spring blooming within. The charred heart she had, one Faelan denied the state of, had begun to warm into living flesh once again, like blueberries springing from the soil after the field had burned.

Faelan disappeared into a wagon. Her muscles tensed and she readied to pounce from her towering vantage point. When he reemerged with a dagger in his hand, her muscles relaxed again. The first seemed to be a wagon stocked with weapons and he had reclaimed one of his own—no Gueritac had been in it. But in which wagon had Mercy been stashed?

Suddenly Angel froze and her knuckles turned pale. She could do nothing. Nothing at all. She had promised to stay out of sight unless *Faelan* was in danger. It was not Faelan in danger. She could do nothing but watch Ipsah's pink wings tremble between two wagons and out of sight.

She prepared for the fight which was sure to follow, propping herself in a position which would allow her to drop to the ground in an instant. But the instant she needed did not come as soon as she thought. For three full minutes she remained stationary, unable to do or see anything of consequence. Then Ipsah's wings reappeared and crept back toward the woods.

"Halt!"

The Gueritac's voice boomed so loud, even Angel felt threatened by the sound. The pink wing began to run. She did not make it three steps before being stopped.

Ranger could do nothing. He kept his stature and place. Faelan, he likely knew, had failed, and he would attempt to trade his 'prisoners' for Mercy. Faelan crept toward Ipsah as fast as invisibility allowed, but he would never make it in time.

Angel would have leapt into this fight and pried Ipsah from the fae's cold severed hand. But she had not promised for Ipsah. She could not enter the Gueritac's sight.

She did not need to.

A brilliant blanket of light covered the camp. It must have been Kaiya's magic, for the light shimmered every shade of the rainbow. Not a soul moved of the Gueritac's group. None of Ranger's group moved either. Only Ipsah moved among the statuesque figures. She ran to Faelan and tugged at his arm. The light which shimmered over everyone else faded from Faelan and he followed her in bewilderment.

Now Angel dropped from her position and hurdled toward the camp, snagging Dorsey's reigns as she ran. The moment she caught Ipsah's eye she scowled.

"Ipsah. Up. You have to ride Dorsey. They'll be looking for you as soon as Kaiya's magic wears off."

"I did it." She said breathlessly. "I did the magic."

"It does not matter. The Gueritac will look for you. Dorsey will take you to Habros and we will follow you there."

"I saw your sister."

This made Angel pause. The desire to know of her sister caused tumult in her heart. But she could not let Ipsah be captured by Shodak.

"Tell me later. You *must* get to safety."

Ipsah obeyed now and mounted the horse. Angel slapped Dorsey and the horse broke into a run, darting around trees in the basic direction of Habros. Then, tipping her head up she shouted "Sil! Take her to Habros! We need her."

"Who is Sil? What happened?"

Angel turned to Faelan. "No time. Come with me." She grabbed his hand and dragged him to the tree she had just vacated. "Climb."

He did as he was told, though his form was too clumsy to accomplish such a task quickly. Her chest thudded in the most horrible, frightening way as she waited for him to get at a height sufficient to prevent his being seen, following him with all the agility her injured arm allowed, fearing a Gueritac would come at any moment and alert the others of their presence.

But no such thing happened. Both elf and halfling sat safely in the upper branches of the tree before the colored light began to dim.

"Angel, what happened?"

"I am not certain." Angel replied, watching the Gueritac closely. "There is magic on the camp keeping them from moving. Ipsah said she did it, but she is a pink wing. She is not strong enough for such magic."

"Kaiya is."

"But Kaiya is frozen too."

Faelan gasped and focused his eyes on the group. She looked too, seeing the same thing she had before. No one blinked, no one breathed and no one made a sound. They looked like statues.

"What happened?"

Angel wished to know the same thing, but a flash of light prompted her to watch the Gueritac. The shimmering blanket evaporated and the Gueritac stared in shock at the pink-wing's disappearance. Ranger's appearance was impatient and indignant. Shodak pointed to various fae and centaurs and sent them in all directions, keeping a dozen fae at the camp and disappearing into one of the wagons.

"Hand me your dagger." Angel said.

Faelan obeyed and she stuck the sheathed knife between her teeth. Then, watching the direction of the centaur-riding Gueritac, she climbed from branch to branch in preparation for their passing.

She heard hoofbeats. She unsheathed the dagger, chose the moment, and dropped on the Gueritac's shoulders. The knife did her bidding and his life left him before he could sound a cry of alarm. She tossed his body aside and took the centaur girl's reigns.

"What is your name?"

"Delyth."

"It is nice to meet you Delyth. I need your help and I cannot waste time. Can you take two riders to Habros without catching the attention of any Gueritac?"

"Yes."

"Are you willing?"

"Yes."

"Even if you do not immediately receive freedom, with only the promise of freedom after our mission is complete, you are willing to help us?"

"A false promise of freedom is better than the true promise of slavery. Have the second rider climb upon my back. I will do the rest."

"Faelan!" She whispered. "Come down."

She had not needed to call him. He was already on the ground. When they reached him, he paused.

"Wait." Faelan said. He reached up and tugged at the reigns. It did not take him ten seconds to remove them and toss them beside the dead Gueritac. Only then did he climb upon Delyth's back.

A new feeling touched Angel's consciousness. The moment Faelan removed Delyth's leather bounds she had brightened like the sun after coming from behind the clouds. As she galloped further away from the Guertiac, she tossed her arms out and touched the saplings and moss and tree bark. She caught a bit of lichen and placed it in her mouth. Though Angel could not see Delyth's expression, she knew it to be the purest, most beautiful expression sweet freedom could offer.

*Please.* Angel thought. *Kaiya, please get my sister out. She deserves sweet freedom too. Sweet freedom from me.*

# Chapter Ten

Pure, wise, glorious freedom! As the heart flies away from its bindings and pursues the simple desires it always longed to enjoy, the beauty it gives to those who watch cannot be fathomed.

But Faelan didn't watch it. He *felt* it.

Every motion of the centaur girl's back, every micro-motion of her arms, and every flick of her hair conveyed the sense of complete and utter release. The leather straps that caused her lacerations and discomfort would forever be absent from her sight. She had left her rider dead in the dust, carrying two creatures who promised her freedom whilst trusting she would not run away. She would not be tethered or beaten, she would be allowed to roam and return as she pleased. She was free.

Ytoran had been the same way.

A flash of pink scraped the wooded scenery. Ipsah.

"Delyth." He yelled. "There is a fairy over there. We need to bring her with us."

"I see her. Why do you need her?"

"She is our friend."

The centaur lady changed her direction. Faelan would have told her more, but a certain circumstance had caught his eye.

Ipsah's position had not changed. She wasn't moving. She lay slumped forward on Dorsey's back, unconscious.

Faelan leapt from Delyth's back and ran toward the horse, but Angel whistled and Dorsey galloped in the halfling's direction. She grasped Dorsey's reigns and motioned for Faelan to join her.

"I believe we should get faerie help for her. Climb here upon Delyth's back and I shall help you get Ipsah on. I will ride Dorsey from here."

He obeyed, and the effort of both creatures resulted in Ipsah being draped over Delyth's breadth. Faelan sat behind her, ensuring she wouldn't fall. Angel climbed on Dorsey and the horse seemed pleased to have its usual rider back.

She looked stunning.

Black horse, black clothing, and black wings created an intimidating and mysterious sight. When she bid Delyth to follow her, her eyes gleamed like pools of mercury. And then—or did he imagine it?—her lips turned upward and sparks shone within her. But before he could separate the real from the imaginary, Delyth galloped after the halfling, forcing Faelan to concentrate on Ipsah and keep her from falling.

Then Habros was before them. He leapt from the centaur girl's back and took Ipsah into his arms. Angel joined him.

"Healer Faelan, come with me. Delyth, stay here and wait for a white-maned centaur and a larger group of faeries."

The centaur girl bowed. "As you wish."

Faelan would have thanked her, but he had no time. He had to keep up with Angel. He ran to the nearest house and Angel, having run faster due to her unburdened arms, knocked.

The door opened and closed before they could speak a single word.

"They do not like me." Angel said. "We must take the appearance of her servants, not her friends, if we wish to be admitted. Come."

She moved to the next house and knocked. Faelan attempted to keep a calm countenance. When the door opened, Angel bowed.

"Sir." She said. "My mistress is ill. She needs faerie medical care, a thing which we cannot give."

The man behind the door scowled and pointed to a large building nearer the center of town. "The pastor will help you. He and his wife are of the healing clan."

"Thank you, sir." Angel said, bowing deeper as the door slammed in her face. Turning to Faelan she said "I am sure you see why my family was despised."

"I don't think I do."

She did not seem to hear him. Her dark form had already made it a third of the way to the church. He ran to catch up and reached her just as she knocked on the church door.

"They won't be in there." He said. "They'll be in the parsonage. There."

She groaned and knocked on that door. A fae appeared and Faelan dropped to his knee, head bowed.

"Sir." Faelan said. "I am a missionary. I beg any aid you are able to give my friends and I. You will be paid if—"

"Faelan?"

He straightened at his name. He looked, for the first time, at the fae's face. With red wings and red hair, this fae's identity could not be mistaken. "Blood?"

"Faelan, how did you get those cuts on your wrists? Who..." He stared at Angel. "Dark Angel? Is that really you? Kaiya told me to expect company today, but—"

"Blood!" Faelan repeated. "I have a fairy, she needs healed. Can you not see her?"

The fae blinked again then pulled the door as wide as its hinges would allow. "I'm sorry. Come in. Come in! Heart! Our company is more distinguished than we thought!"

A pink-winged fairy rushed from an adjoining room, then paused, her hands halfway finished smoothing her hair. "Faelan? Dark Angel? What do you need? Oh, bring the pink-wing this way."

Faelan followed her without hesitation and Angel followed silently. She seemed stunned. Was it so shocking to be treated well by faeries? Or did she wonder at Blood's claim? He had no time to tell.

Heart led them into a small room and directed Faelan to lay her down. "Do you know what caused this?"

"I believe," Angel said "That she suffers magical fatigue. She claimed, before she passed out, that she had frozen an entire campsite with her magic."

Heart stared. "That is not possible. She is a pink-wing—she is not capable of magic like that."

"Which is why I fear it is magical fatigue." Angel asserted.

Heart pursed her lips, then touched Ipsah's wings with a glowing pink fingertip. "She *does* appear to have some fatigue. But I think it is mostly shock. It will not take much to treat her."

The pink-winged healer began pulling some herbs and bottles from the cabinet, sorting them on the counter with expert motions. She kept far more herbs than he could carry. He wanted a place like this.

"Heart! Faelan! Come quick!"

Blood's cries caused both creatures to bolt for the door, and saw him again with the front door opened, holding a fairy with pink-painted wings in his arms.

"Kaiya!"

She lifted her head, brown curls of hair hiding half her face. "Faelan. Where's Ipsah? Are you okay?" She trembled, and Faelan rushed to her side, though Blood kept her steady. "Don't worry about me. Just help me sit down, and I'll be fine."

Heart was also at Kaiya's side, and placed her hand on a pink-painted wing. "Magical fatigue. We need to worry more for Kaiya than for Ipsah."

*** 

In the pandemonium that followed, much managed to be done and little said. They scrubbed the pink paint from Kaiya's wings and put a peppermint-infused fermented berry juice in its place. Heart and Angel removed the tighter garments from both fairies and gave Kaiya a glass of warm milk. She fell asleep a few minutes later.

Only after these things had been completed did anyone take notice of Ytoran. Ranger, they discovered, had sent him ahead after Kaiya collapsed. The others would arrive later—without Mercy.

When all their information had been exchanged Delyth began to converse with Ytoran. As the centaurs wandered away, Faelan and Angel were left to wait for the others in the town square. The air got cooler and Angel leaned into him for warmth. He marveled at her familiarity, and then wondered about her knowledge.

"Angel, I still do not know what magical fatigue is."

Her fingers tightened around the fabric of his shirt, putting painful pressure on his back.

*I heal you, you heal me.*

"The strength of a faeries' magic depends on the amount of magic their wings are able to reproduce in a given period of time. If a fairy uses too much magic, she gets weak and her store of magic is fatigued—but it can be restored after resting. Sometimes the magic fatigue is so extreme it causes something known as magical depletion, in which case a faerie or halfling will never be able to use magic again. They have none left to use."

He heard rawness in her voice. "How do you know this?"

"It happened to Mercy once."

"Fatigue or depletion?"

She sighed. "Depletion."

"Why?"

She drew her arms in, holding them between his body and hers for warmth. "I would not be here if not for her sacrifice. We *must* release her."

"We will." He said. "We will."

Angel sighed. "You do not know that for certain."

"No." He admitted. "I know nothing for certain. No one does."

The sun dipped behind the trees and the town's chickens flocked back to their roosts. Ranger still had not arrived. How much longer would they have to wait?

"Heart and Blood seem to know you." He said.

"They know *you* as well." She growled.

"True." He said. "But I have reason to know them. I fought with them against Isana. We became good friends. How did *you* meet them?"

"When you were busy elsewhere, Blood spoke to me. He said 'Faelan may be wearing a shirt and a cloak, but lashes are visible on his neck and jaw. He and I are brothers, are we not?' You are brothers—brothers of bloodshed."

"He...he never told me about that. You released him?"

She nodded. "At the time, I still released faerie captives. Mercy does still, but I do not. Had your Healing Clan friends not pursued us after the battle, I would not be here."

"Are you almost killed often?"

"Yes." She said. "I sit on the cliff between life and death as often as I sit on the cliff between good and bad. But if someone must die, I would rather it be me."

"I would not let you die for me."

Her silvery eyes stared into his. "I do not want you to die."

A bird chirped in the distance, trilling a sweet tune to the moon. When it quieted, only the stars could be heard. Angel shifted her position away from him.

"Ranger will be here soon. We have only a brief wait."

"He's taken long enough."

Angel shrugged. "He had no choice. He had to bring the thieves with him."

"True." Faelan said. Then he put his arm around Angel's shoulders and pulled her in closer. "There is no need for you to move away. Stay close. Stay warm. Stay alive."

Her arms settled around him and she rubbed her head against his shoulder. "I will, Healer Faelan. I will."

***

The leader rubbed his temples. The wretched monster! He had been unable to shake her. He had been unable to wrench anything useful from her. She sat tall and unbroken, and still not talking.

The halfling's stubbornness had left him desirous of plunging a sword through her black heart. But if he killed her, he would have no chance at Dark Angel. The image of *two* hideously mangled halflings kept the sword far from his hand.

The creature's pale eyes turned upon him, hints of a smirk turning up her black lips. Did she know his fears? Did she believe, as he did, his followers might soon oust him and elect another leader?

He did not know this for sure, but he heard their whispers. He sensed their doubt. Their allegiance to him lasted only as long as his ability to provide ample coin. Without slaves, they would not have as much as they wished, and they would overthrow him regardless of his skills.

"What happened?" The halfling asked. "Did the invader get away?"

He growled. "The fae was drunk—he only imagined he had caught an invader. Scouts were sent after she disappeared and they did not find her. That confirms it was a hallucination."

"Did they all return?"

He struck her with his foot. "Filthy beast! Do you think to doubt me? Do you also doubt my ability to hook Dark Angel like a fish?"

"No."

This word startled him. He thought, for a moment, she had realized his power. But the smirk upon her face wiped that thought away and replaced it with rage. "What do you think then? You are a monster; let us hear your hideous thoughts."

"I do not doubt your ability to capture Dark Angel," the halfling replied, "because I *know* you cannot capture Dark Angel. You are a net flung out to catch the wind. You set your eyes on a target which only a foolish creature could desire."

His hand struck her cheek, but she barely winced from the blow. "She is real. She is solid. She is not the wind. I will capture her and both of you shall die."

"We shall die." The halfling replied, "But not in your hands. Your inability to capture her is due to your reason."

"What does that mean?"

Her piercing eyes dug into him. "Your desire is unworthy. Your desire is revenge. What did she do to cause such hatred?"

He growled. "Dark Angel is the enemy of every Gueritac. I would be celebrated beyond belief if I were the one to stomp out the little nuisance."

"I do not believe you."

"It does not matter what you believe." He said, striking her with his hand again. "When I have her, you will die. Your beliefs matter to no one."

But he could no longer bear her words. His sense of power had diminished more from her than his followers. He would not let it diminish anymore.

Exiting the wagon, he summoned his followers to him. "Come, I have a plan. You wish for captives to sell, we shall have them. Yonder is a town none other has dared to plunder. We shall be the first."

General doubt filled his followers, but he built on their confidence and pride. He assured them the myths were false and the young folk of the town were ripe for the picking. He prodded them with the hope of glorious rewards. He succeeded in stabilizing his leadership. But the length of his reign would be determined by their success in plundering the town of Callamoon.

# Chapter Eleven

The warmth of breaths upon her cheek kept her still. The healer had not let her leave him. He let her lean on his shoulder through the night. He kept her close and warm. He would sleep with her warmth next to him until he awoke.

For hours they remained awake on the floor of the infirmary. He sat with his arm around her and she with her head leaned against his shoulder. He had refused any other position. They had both wanted to remain awake, so they talked and watched Ranger sleeping on the floor.

What a love Kaiya had! His unhesitating willingness to throw himself in front of a battleaxe for her had nothing to do with his inability to be harmed by such weapons. He loved her truly and deeply and would prove it whenever a blade or bludgeon threatened her wellbeing.

Angel would do the same thing for Mercy.

And Edan.

And Faelan.

Puritan said she valued revenge above all other things—even her family. But she did not. She had realized the moment she discovered Mercy's capture that she would not allow Mercy to continue. She would send Mercy the same way Edan had gone. Mercy would not suffer for the choices she made. She would bear her consequences alone.

Why she would give Faelan her life, however, she could not tell. If asked, she would reply that she owed him too much—her life would be a just payment. But she could also say his goodness had won her heart. She valued him above herself. For him, she would do anything.

Voices had been the cause of her awakening, but she had ignored them up to this point. They had said nothing to tempt her otherwise. When she heard her name, however, she found cause to listen.

"They look so peaceful." Heart said. "Let's not wake them."

"Alright." Blood agreed. "But let us keep our important conversations until they are with us."

"Agreed."

Kaiya! She had woken. Ipsah was with them too, as Angel heard her breathing. They had regained much of their strength too; she could hear it in Kaiya's voice.

The faeries talked some more as they gathered a few things. Kaiya draped a blanket over them, worried they would be cold or uncomfortable it their odd position. Their backs and necks would be stiff when they awoke. But she did not try to rouse them, and Angel maintained her position until the door clicked shut, signaling the evacuation of all faeries from the premises.

She opened her eyes and glanced around the room. Not a creature remained. But Kaiya had been right to worry of stiff necks, for she now realized the discomfort her position had caused. Faelan would have the same trouble if she left him thus. She lowered his head into her lap and draped the blanket over him.

Her fingers combed strands of his hair that had fallen loose from his braid. She did wish to loosen his neck muscles, but he might wake up if she tried. She wanted him to sleep.

A bit of color caught her eye, and moving his braid aside, a flower-shaped ring became visible. The magic trinket! He had braided it into his hair. It had so wonderfully escaped the notice of the thieves that it had never been removed from his possession. But she would not allow him to be in the society of such creatures again. He needed not hide his precious ring.

Unbraiding his hair, she removed the ring and slid it on his finger. Then she ran her fingers through the loosed hair, curling the ebony waves around her fingers as it pleased her to do so.

What friends he had! Faeries of every color wing found his life valuable. They even crossed the oceans for her, for his sake. No faerie or elf had done such things for her. Or had these creatures not been acting solely for Faelan. Could they have been doing those good things...*for her*?"

His head shifted position and her fingers paused mid-curl. He settled back down, still sleeping. Did she wish him to catch her in such affectionate gestures?

Years had turned defensiveness and hostility into habit. In her dealings with Faelan, she made a conscious effort to be pleasant, and even then she had been considered hostile. But would the affection in touching his long, unbraided hair be more than he considered appropriate? What if he awoke?

What if he awoke? Would he find it a tender action and return it with equal tenderness? Or would he be appalled and draw away? Still, she curled the black strands around her fingers as it gave her pleasure. She would take what contentment she could from this innocent activity.

His hair was so much longer than hers. For the purpose of battle both she and Mercy had kept their braids at six inches. Now Angel desired hair as long as this elfin healer possessed. She wished for three feet of full, black hair to fall over her shoulders—hair for him to run his hands through.

His hand moved, pushing drowsily at some hair near his ear. She saw the lock he desired to move and placed it in a less annoying position. Then, running her fingers along his jaw, rough scabs scraped her fingertips.

This prompted new action, and she moved aside his cloak. It took several moments of trying before she could pull his shirt up enough to get a look at his back, but when she did she saw the jipanti weed had done its work. The bruises were gone. Only scabs remained.

Her fingers returned to their task of combing the healer's hair, but her mind remained on his marred skin. He had told her the reason for these lashes. She had considered it foolish. But now the reason swelled before her in the sweetest sense. She understood. For the first time, she understood.

It was love.

For a moment, she could hear the strains of a song issuing forth from battered souls. Faelan's glorious voice led strains of praise, ringing through a procession of shattered dreams. He had been their hope. He had loved them all.

Angel rubbed her arm to regain some warmth. A shiver had passed through her as the lyrics filled her mind. But the shiver felt good, like a cool bath on a hot day. Like the hand resting upon her own.

"Healer Faelan." She said, removing her hand from his reach. "How long have you been awake?"

He rose, looking at her with his warm, dark eyes. "Not long. Where are the others?"

"Outside. I woke as they left. I believe Kaiya wished to scour the forest."

"Sounds like her." He said. Then he touched his loose hair. "Did you do this?"

Her cheeks warmed. "Forgive me, I-"

"No need for apologies." He said, leaning toward her. "There is no harm done. But why did you do it?"

She scowled. "You said there is no harm done. My reasons may remain my own."

He smiled. "Do you recall what I told you about me?"

"There is much you have said. Do you expect me to recall all of it?"

"No." He replied. "But I expected you to recall that I am a padparadscha. I can see through you."

"I believed you finished with my character study." She growled.

"I was." He admitted. "But occasionally you surprised me and forced me to reevaluate you."

She scowled again, but turned her face away. Perhaps hiding her eyes would hide what little of the truth he had not seen. "And what, pray tell, do you see?"

"I see decision." He said. "You said you didn't know what you wanted, but you've figured it out. You know what you want. Faeries and elves alike have rejected you and made you believe your desires impossible. *They* are impossible. You *can* love me. I *will* love you back."

She hid her eyes more completely. "You will love me only the way you love Ipsah—as a sister and a friend. You will not..."

"Angel."

The way he spoke caused her to look. His eyes shone and a strand of hair touched his cheek. She brushed the hair away. Her insides collapsed.

"Do not waste your charm on me. You are good at making creatures hope, but it will not work on me. I know the truth."

"And what," He said "is the truth?"

"I am ugly. I am a halfling. You deserve a lovely elfin girl. I do not wish you to spend time on me when there are many elfin girls who would want you."

"Angel."

"I owe you too much."

He touched her hand. "You owe me nothing."

"But I must give you something for all you have given me."

"What have I given you besides a few stitches? What have I offered but to heal your wounds, which you repaid by healing mine? What have I given you that is more valuable than what you have given me?"

"You cannot know what you have given me."

"Then I cannot know why you must repay me. If you must give me something, Angel, give me trust. Believe me when I say you are beautiful, you deserve every bit of charm I give, and no elfin girl has made me feel half so deeply as you. Believe me and I will be repaid, for to be accused of lying is great punishment to me."

She bowed her head. "I will only owe you more."

"No, Angel. Only believe me truthful. Know that I will never lie to you. Angel, please listen to me."

"I am listening." She choked. "I hear your every word. But why must you pain me with your goodness? Why must you tell me these things? If you speak true, why does it pain me?"

"You said you cannot always feel pain. But why the truth pains you, I don't know. You have felt so little...perhaps it hurts to feel more."

She leaned into his chest, letting him encircle her with his arms. She moved her fingers through his hair. She took comfort in his beating heart. She allowed herself to believe his words. "You will never leave."

"That's right." He said. "I will never leave."

She relaxed in his arms and he kissed her forehead. Then his lips touched hers and she would not allow them to be taken away. He had no objections to this and after she released him he held her tenderly in his arms for several minutes before she declared finding Kaiya a necessity. Angel would have spent the whole day with Faelan had not Mercy's situation been so contrary to hers. To release Mercy would be her priority. To die saving Mercy seemed her only way to give Faelan the life he deserved.

# Chapter Twelve

"You're awake!" Kaiya called, waving through skeletal branches. "How did you find us?"

"I just followed the big purple blob jumping from tree to tree." Faelan replied. "You don't exactly blend in."

"Unlike you two." Kaiya giggled. "Ranger still hasn't seen you and he's only over there."

Faelan glanced the direction she pointed. "Have you thought of a plan to rescue Mercy?"

Kaiya shook her head. "We've been waiting for you two. You were sleeping so peacefully—"

"You didn't want to wake us." Faelan called back. "Are you going to come down?"

Before he could blink Kaiya was on the ground and walking towards them. "Of course. Now, I want to hear everything you know—and don't worry about *them* not hearing it. I'll make sure they get filled in. Come on."

Kaiya hooked Angel's arm and pulled. Faelan ran after them, listening to Angel's words—few though they were—and confirming he had done no more than what Angel described. In short, neither had anything valuable to offer.

But Ipsah did. When she saw them she leapt from her seat and threw her arms about Faelan's neck, pouring forth her story in deafening excitement as the healer tried to free himself from her grip.

"Ipsah! Calm down. You are breaking my eardrums."

A sudden jerk freed him from the pink-wing's grasp. Taking in two breaths, he saw Ipsah's stunned face and Angel's heated glare upon the fairy.

"Do not embrace him. His back still pains him."

Guilt overtook Ipsah's face, and she shrunk to a lump on the grassy ground. Faelan's conscience prodded him to comfort her, but he wondered if it might seem like flirting. Jealousy lived in Angel's glare.

"It's alright, Ipsah." He said. "It doesn't hurt very much, but it is tender. I would like to avoid hugs for a while. Please, I'm anxious to hear of your adventures."

It took no further prodding for her to start spilling the words all over again—this time without causing breakage to Faelan's eardrum.

"I was worried about you and followed you in—but I didn't know which wagon you went into—so I went into one and I saw" She pointed at Angel "A halfling that looked almost *exactly* like you. I tried to untie her but she told me I'd wreck the plan and told me to deliver a message to Angel, Kaiya and Ranger—"

"How does she know about them?"

Ipsah's cheeks turned the shade of her wings. "I might have said something about it...anyways, she said for Ranger, Kaiya, Angel and I to fly ahead to the Castle Callamoon at noon. The rest of you are to follow at sunset—and arrive at about midnight."

"But when the Gueritac caught you," Faelan said, "How did you escape?"

She bit her lip. "I'm not quite sure about that. I mean, I think I did the magic, but..." She shrugged. "I don't know."

He kept watching her. She seemed nervous, unsure, worried. Her lower lip remained between her teeth and she twirled her hair around her finger absently, wishing someone would think of something helpful or definite, but unable to make any suggestions herself.

Then he saw it.

The answer.

Bolting to her side, he grasped her forearm and twisted her hand to reveal a delicate trillium imprinted on her palm. As he stared at it, the red and white shone unnaturally pure, then faded into flat colors again.

"I don't believe it."

Kaiya inched forward, still unable to see what he could. "What?"

He couldn't speak. Something he had considered harmless suddenly became, before his eyes, something frightening and dangerous. Why couldn't he have done something else?

"Faelan, what is it? What can you not believe?"

"A connection."

No one seemed to understand what he meant. He released Ipsah's arm and looked down at the ring. Angel had taken from his hair and placed upon his finger. He removed it, holding it delicately out to Angel.

"Take it. You can do no harm with it."

"Faelan!" Kaiya said, snatching his arm and forcing him to look at her. "What do you mean? Explain it to me! Please!"

"I cannot fully explain." He replied. "I only know that because I imprinted Ipsah with the image of your blood, your magic travels to it without limit. It weakens you more than direct magic ever would."

"That doesn't mean you have to get rid of the ring." Kaiya said. "Even Terrwyn, the first of the Hero Clan, didn't have enough magic for this. But it's important. Keep the ring. You'll be more careful in the future."

He looked into her emerald eyes—eyes greener than his blood— and spoke quietly. "I have more reason than that for her to have it, Kaiya."

The eyes widened and her hand loosened its grip on his arm. "The fate of the ring is your choice." She said. "Is this your choice?"

He bowed his head. "This is my choice."

Kaiya released his arm and he placed the ring in Angel's hand, closing her fingers around it. "When you leave, wear this. I will not see you for twelve hours after we part."

She shook her dark head. "I cannot fly ahead with Kaiya and Ranger. I cannot fly at all."

He smiled, squeezing her hand gently. "I know. That is why you must wear the ring. Kaiya's magic will help you fly—all you have to do is wear her blood on your finger."

Both creatures now looked down at the ring, seeing the crimson lines and green sepals on the flower, knowing it to be more than the gems most would see them to be. Love was the color of blood. What ornament could be more beautiful than that?

"Very well." She replied. Her voice held habitual indifference, but her eyes shone with tenderness. "The matter is settled. Let us prepare to leave."

***

The sun stood in the center of the sky. An earthy breeze passed over the landscape. Most of the townspeople bolted from here to there, trying to get their work done. They had no time to appreciate the sweet smell offered by the cool winds.

But Faelan did. Six hours from now he would be setting out to follow the four faeries. All preparations had been finished and the Healing Clan couple had given him leave to do as he pleased. It pleased him to turn toward the breeze, soaking every sense in the shifting air as it passed.

It smelled like Angel. Earthy and pungent and sweet. But the wind did not have her warmth. It had no words to speak or lessons to teach. It smelled like Angel, but nothing could replace her.

He turned to the sun and noted its distance from the horizon. An hour had passed, and five hours more he would wait. He could not understand Mercy's reason for separating them. Wouldn't it have been safer to send them together? Ytoran and Delyth could have kept up with the faeries.

But why would Mercy divert them to a castle when they were already at her side? Why had she sent them away?

Had they been deceived?

# Chapter Thirteen

Angel could not believe it. In the space of ten minutes, they had covered the galloping distance of eight hours. Never had she travelled so fast before. And never again. Faeries were made to fly when they came of age. She was not.

But Mercy would have enjoyed this. Her eyes had forever been upon the sky. Her dreams and hopes had belonged to the life of a fairy. She had not. Oh, how she would have loved flying high above the treetops with the wind whipping her hair about! She would have felt closer to God than ever before. She would have been happy.

The ground rose and they swerved to prevent a collision with a mountain. By the time the ground dropped again, their descent had begun. Their glittering goal awaited them.

The Castle of Callamoon.

It shone violet in the sunlight, sparkling as though a million amethysts covered its walls. Cows grazed on the hillsides without a care, lifting their heads for only a moment as the foreign creatures passed overhead. Gardens ran along the banks of the stream, promising vegetables galore in the summer months, but now laying dormant in the cold atmosphere. What a lovely place this would be to live!

Three faeries landed and Angel collapsed. Her limbs shook so hard she could do naught but lay on the grass, thanking God for a solid surface to rest upon.

"Angel, get up! We're not there yet."

The halfling attempted to raise her head, but she could not. She did, however, manage to speak. "We are not there, but I ache from top to toe. How can your magic be so excruciating?"

Kaiya laughed. "I never said the transformation was painless— besides, I only lengthened your wings to keep you in the air. They're back to normal now."

Angel growled, but could not rise. The 'lengthened wings' had hurt enough, but Kaiya had been forced to control Angel's wings with her magic and, not having nerve connections to Angel, she had not realized the suffering her shoulder had caused. It hurt too much to move.

"Is your friend okay?"

The growling depth of the voice startled the halfling. She almost accomplished a kneeling position before collapsing on the ground again. In the few moments she had been upright, she had seen enough.

The creature who asked of her wellbeing was a dragon. Smoke trickled from its nostrils and sharp teeth protruded from its jaw like an oversized crocodile. If she had been strong, she would have drawn her sword, but it would have been a pathetic move. No sword could match a dragon's scales.

"She'll be alright." Kaiya said. "She just doesn't like flying. Do you know how we can rescue Mercy? What is the castle made of? It looks like the walls are constructed from—"

"Hush." The dragon said. "It will all be explained later. Can she walk?"

Angel could do naught but groan. Though she disliked needing help, she had come to realize when she needed it. She needed it now, even if a dragon was the one to offer it.

"I can carry her."Ranger said, crouching.

"No, Ranger." Kaiya said. "You'll need your arms free. Come, Angel. I'll carry you to the castle."

"Very well." She said, rising some. Kaiya's arms took her up and carried her toward their destination.

Fifty feet of dragon walked alongside them, its scales as black as the blood in her veins. Bulbous eyes as yellow as the sun glanced back on occasion, observing their progress. The dragon had no wings but had enormous feet, and could have been back at the castle before they took their first two steps.

But this beast trod alongside them in silence until they stood a dozen yards from the castle gate. At that point, it stood in their way, leveling its black head with Angel's.

"I must warn you." The dragon growled. "This castle is no ordinary fortress. All who enter its gates see their true selves. You cannot hide iniquity. You take the shape of the creature your character resembles most. Take this as warning or encouragement, but the effect lasts only as long as you are within those walls. Do you still wish to enter?"

"Yes." Kaiya replied, dismounting from her horse. "I am not afraid of being seen through. I see through you plenty well."

Ranger and Ipsah echoed Kaiya's affirmation. Angel did not.

What went through her head could not be described, but the mixture of emotions and imaginations showed through on her face as tiredness and confusion. This led Kaiya and Ranger both to believe she had not been listening. They repeated the question to her, and now required to give an answer, she gave the only true answer she could.

"I care not, so long as I may save Mercy."

Before Angel knew to prepare herself, she was at the gate. The dragon turned its yellow eyes upon her, looking curiously into her eyes. Then the monster leapt through a wall of violet light.

Angel forgot all her hesitation for, as the dragon disappeared, a fae with black dragon tattoos winding up his body landed hands and knees on the other side of the castle gate. The fae rose, turned, and bowed to the outsiders.

"I am the Taferi, the Dragon of Callamoon. I see you have already met my wife."

This caught Angel's attention, for she had met no one. Ranger and Kaiya glanced at Angel before turning their eyes upon Ipsah. Ipsah, a creature of timidity and gentleness, was the only unattached female present. But the timidity had dropped as a curtain from her face, and she stood with her neck straight, unafraid to make eye contact.

"Ipsah?" Kaiya said. "You are married? You tricked us? Why have you *really* brought us to Callamoon?"

The pink-wing smiled, blushing. "I *am* married, and I tricked you only in my identity. We *are* here to help Mercy. But we are here for many other reasons." Ipsah's gaze turned to Ranger and she curtsied. "King Charranger, I would like to thank you—you married the girl who killed my sister."

What caused Ranger to tremble could not be discerned from Angel's viewpoint, nor could she determine why his face turned paler than sheep's wool. She only watched as Taferi held out a hand and Ipsah placed her hand in it, walking through a shower of violet light.

Still pink-winged, she stood beside Taferi, but her face would never have been recognized. She did not resemble Ipsah at all. She actually looked like Ranger.

Ranger trembled and tears trailed down his cheeks. He moved his lips, but he made no sound. He swallowed deliberately before he managed one strangled word. "Jakie."

She laughed. "You remember me!"

Ranger bolted through the gate and his arms had wrapped about the fairy. As the tears ran down his cheeks, Ranger uttered some words that stunned the only one present who did not know what was happening.

"I thought you were dead, Jakie. I thought I'd lost you. My dear sister, you have no idea how I have missed you."

Ipsah was Ranger's *sister?*

# Chapter Fourteen

God had returned Ranger's sister to him. Why He took her in the first place could be debated until every face turned blue and the debaters dropped dead from exhaustion. No one would ever come to a conclusion. But the paths which had been taken led to joyful lives independent of the siblings thought to be lost. The circuitous course might only have been a Creator's way of making all the ends tie together in one beautiful knot.

Kaiya passed Angel to Taferi as she stepped through the gate. Ipsah had been Jakayla all along, yet only Taferi had known. Why? For what reason had she hid from her brother? How had she changed her appearance to one so unlike her own? The questions piled up so deep that when Ranger released her from the embrace, Kaiya couldn't hold them any longer.

"Why didn't you tell the truth from the start? How did you survive Isana's attack? Who controls this castle? What—"

"Hush, Kaiya." She said, laughing. "I want nothing more than to answer every question you have and tell you every secret of this castle, but we don't have time for that. I'll tell you what I can, though."

"Please," Ranger said. "Tell me how you escaped Isana. Why didn't you seek me out?"

"To escape Isana, I did only what a Shape-shifter Clan does." She replied. "I healed myself. As to seeking you out...I did not know you were alive until almost a year ago, when you became king. Other things kept me from you then."

She continued to explain how she had fled toward the west, not knowing of its dangers, and been captured by Gueritac. Taferi had seen the Gueritac group and released her. Their marriage followed several months later, and by the time she heard of Ranger's coronation, she wasn't able to travel, as she would have to take her child with her.

Ranger nearly fell over when he heard she had a child. She proudly described the boy as being the most adorable thing, with yellow wings and eyes like his father's. Taferi had such sweet, round eyes in his faerie form; she knew the boy would look just like him.

"But why the deception?" Kaiya asked, after this had been explained. "Why did you not come to us immediately?"

Jakayla bit her lip. "I have wanted to tell you my identity since I first saw you, Kaiya. I wanted it more when I saw Ranger. But I had reasons for my deception. Look at my hand."

Her outstretched palm still held the trillium insignia, its ruby streaks gleaming like gemstones. Kaiya had not had the faith to remove it earlier, and now looked at it with the realization that, perhaps, she had not been meant to.

"I had to fool Faelan into believing me no more than a fellow captive—and a terrified one at that. I had to get this imprint, and I had to show Angel Faelan's tenderness. It is...I will tell more later." She paused, biting her lip again. Though not as timid as her alter ego, she remained tentative and careful of her words. "But the reason I had to get this mark was to prevent you from completing the plan. It would have split Angel and

Faelan up too soon if it had worked—which is the reason I pretended to be unconscious."

"You *pretended* to be unconscious?"

Jakayla chewed at her fingernail. "Yes, but I had no choice. I'm directed by a Higher source, and the directions required me not only to pretend unconsciousness, but cause symptoms of magical fatigue in you."

Relief touched Kaiya. "You mean my magic wasn't fatigued?"

Jakie shook her head. "No. I used the trillium mark to cause symptoms. I can't use it to actually exhaust you. You're too strong and we are blood-related, so-"

"Wait." Kaiya said. "Blood related? But I wasn't blood-related to Isana. How am I blood-related to you?"

Jakie blushed. "Forgive my embarrassment, but I rarely have to give such news as this.—Your throne, Kaiya, will have an heir by the end of next summer."

***

Angel touched her ears. She looked at her hands. She twisted in order to probe her back. She found no wings, useless or otherwise. Her skin had turned a greenish-brown hue. Her ears remained as pointy as a birch's leaf. She had become what she had always desired to be. Oh, what a glorious thing was this magic castle!

If only she could stay here forever. In here she would always appear to be an elf, and she might seem a little more worthy of the elf she desired. But it could not be. She was a monster. Marrying an elf like Faelan should be looked upon with the same disgust as a dragon marrying a faerie.

This reminded her of the dragon-fae, and she found him to be seated on a bench three yards away. His eyes were upon her, and when she took notice of him, he smiled and pointed at the three faeries. "Her name is not Ipsah. It is Jakayla."

"And she is married to a dragon." Angel snarled. "I am a halfling. I know enough of ridicule. What of *your* children? What shall they endure?"

"Less than you." He replied. "There is magic in this castle, it was left for us hundreds of years ago. Every creature in these walls is born being what they should be for the rest of their lives. When they walk out of the castle, nothing changes. As long as my children are born in here, they will be what they are meant to be. Just like your brother."

She scowled. "You are mistaken. I am searching for my sister. I have no brother."

"Oh, but I do not often err in my facts." He said. "My predecessors kept marvelous track of every creature born here, their parents, and whether any children were born to them afterward. It was not difficult to find your name."

"It is none of your business." She snapped. "Besides, he is my half brother, so he cannot be counted."

"He can." The dragon-fae replied. "Your parents fed you the only story they could for such an odd combination of children. His father was your father—he would have been a halfling. But Edan was born here."

"Why would they leave, then?" She snarled. "If they had stayed, their children would not have been ridiculed. We could have been whole instead of partial."

"Callamoon is a resting place, a place to gather up the broken pieces of your life and heal before moving on to accomplish your greater purpose. They had to move on...and your purposes, thus far, would not have been accomplished if they had not. Edan's certainly would not."

"Do you know where he is?" Angel asked. "I want to tell him this."

"You cannot." Tefari said. He pointed to the three faeries. "Ranger believed Jakayla to be dead. Yet she is here, she lives. She only left the belief of her death at Isana's hand, as you believe Edan is alive. The truth is the reverse of what was believed of both."

Angel scowled. "Do not attempt to twist my brain in tangles so thick grief cannot seep through. If you mean to say he is dead, say it clear and tell me what you know."

The dragon-fae sighed. "Ask Kaiya about your brother. She can tell you the story best."

Angel turned her eyes and kept them, for a while, on the three faeries. Ranger's sister, one he thought to be dead, stood alive and talking to them. She lived.

But the reverse caused her pain. If the dragon spoke true, Edan had not only died, but died at the hands of a mercenary queen. Though she had heard little of Isana, she knew the uneven steps Kaiya took were caused by a battle between them. A battle Kaiya had lost.

"Angel."

She glared at the dragon-fae. "You should not be here. You should be with your wife and your new siblings. Leave me in peace."

"I am not with them for a reason. For the first time in three years, my wife can see her brother and talk to his wife as a sister. She does not need me for that. You, however, need someone to teach you the truth."

She glared again and looked away. "What can you to teach me that Faelan cannot?"

"Ah, yes. He has taught you much, and he will teach you more, as you will teach him. But what I have to teach you can be taught by no other. Your beau will not mind."

"You," She choked "Have no right..."

"Do you wish to be worthy of Faelan?"

"What do you infer?"

He looked at her. "Stand up. This castle has a way of refreshing those who come tired and broken."

She rose, as directed. Her muscles no longer throbbed. She crossed her arms and scowled. "If you have something to teach, teach."

He waved his hand toward the grassy portion of the courtyard. "Go look into the pond. Return and tell me what you see."

She obeyed, treading the grassy surface until her toes touched the water. Gazing into its depths, she first saw her face, tinged with green and without wings to draw attention away from her pointed ears. Then her eyes roved the reflection more. Her knees weakened and her fingers moved to touch the things she saw in the pond. Nothing. She did not resemble her reflection. But what did this mean?

The dragon-fae held the answer.

She returned to the bench and collapsed onto it. Glaring at the dragon-fae, she felt the urge to curse him and tell him all the cruel things faeries had heard from her before. But his eyes held kindness similar to Faelan's. Any desire to hurt him dissipated.

"What did you see?"

"I saw a hallucination." She growled. "The image in the water does not reflect me at all."

"But it does." The dragon-fae said. "That pond, like the castle, is magical. In the castle you are shown what you are meant to be. In the pond, you are shown what you are."

The dragon-fae paused, looking at Angel. "Tell me what you saw."

"I saw a reflection of myself." She said, hiding her head. "Except I wore chains about my wrists and ankles, and the wounds that have healed, the scars you see, were open again. It makes no sense. They are healed. They should not seep blood."

"Are your wounds healed?"

"Yes. Only one is open—this one on my shoulder. All others are healed."

"Did you see your shoulder-wound in the pond?"

She paused to consider more carefully what she had seen. "No. Neither shoulder had a wound upon it."

Taferi nodded. "Healers do not only heal the body. It is also their job to heal the soul. Until now, you have let healers do only half of their work."

Her eyes turned to the pond again. "How can I heal myself? How can I close the wounds?"

"You cannot heal yourself." The dragon-fae replied. "And perhaps that is the beauty of it. You consider Faelan too good for you, but for that reason he bends to tend your wounds. He wants to make you worthy of him."

Angel bowed her head. "Then he will be sorely disappointed."

"That depends on whether you let him." Taferi said. Then he stood, looking toward the faeries. "They have had enough time. There is much we would like you to learn about this castle—but one room in particular shall be of interest to you all. Come."

# Chapter Fifteen

Time passed and the sun sank a few more degrees. Faelan worried for Angel's safety. He no sooner thought of a possible answer than another question stabbed through his thoughts. Something wasn't right.

He rubbed his face and let it rest in his hands. For a moment, he wondered why he had let her go. He should have insisted on following, on having Kaiya lend him a pair of wings. But she had been fatigued, and whether she would manage Angel's flight was questionable. He could not ask more of her.

And he could not leave yet. He promised Ipsah he would not leave until the sun dropped behind the trees. If only they had not made him promise.

An image of Angel printed itself on his eyelids, and he did not attempt to wash it away. He wanted to see her. He had been driven mad by his inability to speak with her during the preparations. He wanted to kiss her again and hold her tight in his arms, where he knew her to be safe.

Safe. The halfling he chose should be safe from the Gueritac. Had the Gueritac set a trap for her? Had they forced Mercy to say those things? Had his friends been set up?

A few drops of liquid seeped from his eyes, cleansing the image upon his eyelid. It had taken little time for him to like Angel's appearance. She had been beautiful from the start, though the shade of her skin had taken a few minutes to get accustomed to. He had not noticed it since the first day. But he no longer saw her as a halfling.

She had brown skin, the earthy tones delicately shaded with green. Her eyes remained gray, and her smile...he had seen it so few times, but his mind placed her smile upon her permanent image. Beautiful. His mind had given her an image not physically correct, but one he desired to see. One he knew she would have had, if not for her faerie half.

\*\*\*

Callamoon Castle looked like most other castles from the outside. It had towers and turrets, walls and gates. The courtyard, though small, was eternally green with grass and trees. The windows looked small, but so did the doors. All in all, it looked the same as the castle in Idlerose.

Inside, however, nothing was the same. Stained glass windows stretched the height of the wall, letting glorious rainbows illuminate the room without blinding those who walked along them. There was not a hall or a room without at least one wall of stained glass to allow the illumination of the space. This was remarkable since three-quarters of the rooms were entirely surrounded by other rooms.

Then there was the distance between the rooms. Though the castle had to obey the laws of space and have no more rooms than its area could support, the law of distance was bent. No one ever had to walk further than fifty feet to reach their destination. No one ever tired of walking and no one ever got lost.

Angel learned all this by adhering to Kaiya's side as the queen released a barrage of questions. Taferi answered most of the questions, giving replies quickly and with precision—satisfying Kaiya's curiosity with few words and in little time. This, according to Angel's experience, was no easy task.

It did not take long, however, for Kaiya to begin asking questions about Mercy. The dragon-fae admitted to having a plan, but refused to go into specifics. Angel might have attempted strangling the plan out of him, if not for the words that followed the refusal.

"You are not alone in your desire to rescue Mercy. One of our fae also attempted a rescue. Jas was his name, I believe."

"Jas!"

Taferi paused, his eyes upon her. "Do you know him?"

"Yes. He was betrothed to Mercy. We thought him dead."

"Interesting." Taferi said. "He thought her dead until he heard of her capture. She must still love him because, though he tried to release her and stay in her stead, she refused to go without him."

Water wished to flow from Angel's eyes, but instead of carving rivers upon her cheeks they drilled chasms in her chest. Many years had passed since Mercy had been betrothed. She had been seventeen and glowing with dark beauty. She was now aged twenty-three and almost as scarred, body and soul, as Angel. Yet Mercy still loved him. He still loved Mercy.

"May I speak to Jas?"

Jakie shook her head. "I'm sorry, but he disappeared after his attempt to free her. I can't even find him in the glass."

"The glass?"

The pink-wing smiled. "That is where we are going. Or, rather, it is through this door."

The hickory-wood door to which Jakayla motioned was opened, the dragon-fae bowing as he bid the ladies to enter first.

The room they entered caused Angel to stare in awe. Magic filled the air and breathed life into every corner of the circular room. Stained glass windows stretched five feet above their heads and surrounded them in rainbows of glorious, magical light.

But there was something odd about the windows. In every window, the scene centered upon the same violet-winged fairy. In every window, a figure clad in white stood in the upper corner. In every window, there was a trillium flower.

Angel fiddled with Faelan's ring and wondered. Though the fairy depicted in the windows had hair the color of wheat stalks, and Kaiya's was the shade of wet earth, the trillium symbol seemed an unlikely coincidence. Could Kaiya be the fairy in the windows?

"Oh," Kaiya said, going to the window in the center of the display. "It is like something out of a dream."

Angel agreed. The pane stood taller than all the others and the figure, which was small in all the others, occupied most of the frame. It was a man, holding the fairy in his arms, the blood from his palms staining her clothing yet, somehow, seeming to make it more pure. The fairy's arm hung limp, as though she was unconscious, and she held the stem of a painted trillium delicately in her hand.

"This is Terrwyn's room." Jakie said. "After her husband died, Terrwyn came here to mourn…but she couldn't rest. Her love and grief overflowed into involuntary magical acts, and some feared her magical eccentricities would cause problems. So she channeled all her magical strength on placing a spell on the castle. Over several months the dark chambers became glorious rooms filled with symbols of faith and love, the distance from one end to the other disappeared and, finally, all who entered took their true form. But this" She put her hands over a circle on the floor.

It rose to waist height, turning from stone to clear glass. "This is the glass. Come, look into it."

Angel moved forward, as did her companions. The glass, however, regardless of the direction she looked into it, showed nothing but the colors of the stained glass. Kaiya also saw nothing, as she spoke her inability to Jakie, who laughed.

"I didn't expect you to see anything in it. You are not the seer."

"What do you mean?"

"Terrwyn didn't see everything as clearly as you do. God gave her the ability to create this glass, so that creatures who share her dim vision could see a little farther than the end of their nose. Only one creature in every generation can see what is in the glass, and they are always drawn, in one way or another, to Castle Callamoon."

Kaiya looked at the glass again. "And you are one of those creatures?"

Jakie bowed her head. "I am."

"What do you see?"

Jakie's eyes glowed. "I see the present and the likely course for the future. I see what God wants me to see in order that I may change or keep on track the direction of events by direct or indirect manipulation. I am the string that jerks the limb of living marionettes, tugged by the great Puppeteer as He sees fit. It is my destiny and my delight."

"What of Mercy?" Angel asked, looking harder into the blurred colors of the glass. "What can you see of her?"

"I can see her and where she is, but there is little else to see. I've seen what must be done already."

"What of Faelan, then? Is he travelling yet?"

The pink-wing laughed. "I could tell you the answer by looking out the window. It is not sun-set. He is not on his way yet."

Angel scowled. "Then what am I to do until he arrives? When will we go to save Mercy?"

"Be patient." The pink wing said. "All will happen as it is supposed to happen. We cannot speed things along by rushing headfirst into battles that are not ours to make."

"But she is my sister!"

"I understand." The pink-wing replied. "She is your sister. But there are greater works occurring. She will come out without a scratch, without a scar. She will be fine. Wait a few hours and you will see what I mean."

# Chapter Sixteen

Angel looked around as the halls passed by. The faeries wished to be alone, family as they were, to talk of their lives, passions and plans. Still, they had refused to let Angel wander the castle without another and had called a friend, for they had no servants, to be her companion.

The yellow-wing they chose held little promise of being a companion. She had scarce spoken ten words and, when she chose to utter a syllable or two, her words were unintelligible. They had walked the halls for a quarter-hour now and the girl had not made a sound. Angel would have found a statue more companionable.

But perhaps Taferi had chosen wisely. Angel was in no mood to talk. To obtain peace in the presence of a talkative fairy she would have considered various silencing strategies; gagging, strangulation and molten glares were especially likely to be used in such a venture. None of these measures would have to be taken, however. Taferi had chosen wisely indeed.

Though silence was preferred to endless chatter, the fairy had spoken too little. Angel had the ability to change that. She might heal the breach.

"What is your name?"

The fairy paused, looking at Angel with pale gray eyes. "I cannot speak it within these walls. Please do not ask it of me again."

"Surely there is a name the others in this castle use for you."

"They do not know me yet."

"Then what shall I call you?"

"Why do you care?" The fairy whispered. "You are a legend. You despise faeries and refuse to release them when you have the chance. I have heard much of you. You should not care about a creature like me."

Angel sighed. "If you knew nothing of me, would you still reject me as you do now?"

"I do not reject you." The fairy replied. "But I have seen your works and the pain your hatred has caused. Allow me to ask one question, and promise you will answer truthfully."

"I will answer truthfully."

"If you could start over again, if you could change your actions, would you do it?"

"There are many things I would change. And there are many things that I would change about my behavior. I *have* changed my behavior."

The fairy smiled and resumed walking. "You may call me your companion, the yellow-wing, or whatever pleases you. Would you mind if we were to spend our time in the library?"

"Go where you would like, and I shall follow."

"Why so eager to please me?"

"It has been my experience that creatures are most interesting in places where they enjoy being. I am likely to be far more interesting here than anywhere else in the world."

"I would not know." The fairy replied, pausing to push open a door. "Come, the library waits."

The companions stepped into the room. The immense size of the library rivaled all the rooms she had seen before. Books lined shelves as needles lined a pine's branches. Angel's companion leapt into the branches, climbing their height with celerity, and plucked out a book. The fairy offered to read aloud to the companion she had been assigned.

Angel could not object to this. The quantity of books caused a spark of interest in her mind, for among enormous quantity must be some quality. The two creatures settled in a padded corner of the room and the fairy began reading. The fairy's smooth voice and sweet countenance aroused beautiful memories as the words from the books offered stories and knowledge for her to grasp or disregard as she chose.

She chose to grasp it.

\*\*\*

The remaining hours passed with more haste than the first few, and the companion fairy disappeared among the others as soon as dinner was served. Angel did not realize this at first, as Jakie had stolen her attention with an update on Mercy's condition.

"The Gueritac are coming *here?*"

"Yes." Jakie said. "I cannot be sure exactly when, but they are headed in this direction. Shodak wishes to redeem himself after yesterday's events, and he seems to think attacking us will accomplish that. Which, of course, it won't. He underestimates our powers."

"Powers?"

"Yes, Angel. I may be a pink wing, and Taferi has no magic at all, but we have something magical strength cannot achieve."

"What is that?"

Jakie smiled. "Goodness, moral strength, love, dependence on one another—we are a unit of creatures who have great cause to fight against the Gueritac. We can achieve our goal."

"But-"

"Angel!"

Kaiya rushed over and grabbed her arm. "You're bleeding all over the floor. Come, I'll refresh the bandages. It won't take long."

Before Angel could reply, Kaiya had dragged her out of the dining hall and into a small room. This room had shelves of healing supplies stacked to the ceiling, and Kaiya had no difficulty in choosing the supplies she desired to use.

"Can we not wait for Faelan?"

Kaiya looked at her a moment, then looked back down at the herbs she had measured into a bowl. "Of course not. He won't be here for another five or six hours and your bandage needs changed *now*."

Angel looked at the bandage. The fabric had been soaked with black liquid. It needed changed. She could not dispute it.

"Very well." Angel growled. "Are you also a healer?"

Kaiya smiled. "Not exactly. You might have noticed that I ask a lot of questions, and because I'm friends with Faelan, I was always asking him what he did and why. I'm surprised he didn't get quite annoyed with the younger, less delicate me. Believe it or not, I was a *lot* more curious then. There, you're done."

Angel glanced at the bandages and saw the job to be complete. But she turned her face back to Kaiya and watched with confusion as Kaiya wrapped the soiled bandages in a layer of cloth and tucked it into a bag.

"There is a wash-bucket over there for you to put those in." Angel said, pointing at a water-filled bucket. "You need not carry them around."

"Oh, I do not wish to wash them." Kaiya said, clipping the bag shut. "I have some experiments I would like to try with this. A faerie's blood is one thing, an elf's another...but when they are combined, surely they have some interesting properties."

She could not understand Kaiya's meaning, so Angel growled and returned to the dining hall as swiftly as Kaiya had taken her away. It was nearly twenty minutes before Kaiya returned, bearing no bag of bandages. She must have returned them to her room. Regardless, Angel greeted her and thanked her for changing it—she had neglected to show her gratitude before. Kaiya shrugged and suggested they eat. They would require strength to battle the Gueritac.

But the events of the day had heightened Angel's perception, and she had a vague feeling of uneasiness. Jakie had likened her abilities to being a puppeteer's string, yanking the limb of the marionette as the Puppeteer chose her to do it. How had she yanked Angel's strings? And for what purpose?

***

If anyone had watched Kaiya for the twenty minutes she had been absent, they would have seen her exit the castle gate and meet a fae on the other side. Time will not be wasted in describing his features. He has been described already. Before her was the image of Shodak.

"I can't believe you were..."

"Shh." He said. "Finish your work quickly. I must leave soon."

Kaiya sighed and unwrapped the bandages, using her magic to draw the living blood from its fabric. Then, opening a hole in his arm, she drew blood out from him. The two bloods mixed, black as night, magic from one transferring to the other. The blood from his arm returned to him loaded with whatever magic Angel's had held. The cut sealed, leaving no trace of the incision.

"That should do it." Kaiya said.

"I hope so." He said. "There will be no other chance."

"I know." Kaiya sighed as she reentered the castle gate. "I will see you later. They will get suspicious if I stay out here much longer."

Shodak watched her for a short time, then sank into the shadows. His time was coming. Excitement and dread could not be held back. Until the hour came in which he could be freed, he would remain outside, hidden by darkness and cloaked by night. When morning came, all would be as it should have been.

# Chapter Seventeen

Faelan crashed through some brush, scraping his limbs on their points as he fell. But tripping would not prevent his body from moving forward and his feet resumed pounding the ground only moments later. Though rotten logs collapsed beneath his feet and tree limbs smacked his face, he could not stop. He had to reach the castle.

"Faelan, please! Ride upon my back. You may hurt yourself."

"No." Faelan panted. "You cannot run fast in the dark. I will lead the way."

Ytoran tossed Faelan onto his back, giving the elf no choice but obedience. "I refuse to allow you to injure yourself. I will run faster if necessary, but you shall not arrive beaten to pieces by your own temper."

This made sense, but it made no peace. Raging war within made him desire to make war without. Running had occupied him. Now it did not.

If only he had *insisted* on going with them! He might have been there and not had the war waging within. He could not bear this. Would not bear this.

A birdlike creature landed upon his shoulder. "Your fears are founded. I spotted Shodak outside the castle. By all means, hurry!"

\*\*\*

A tinny sound pierced the air and the smell of blood tainted Angel's nostrils. No drop of blood had been lost yet, but the tinny sound had been explained many hours before. The Gueritac were here.

The sky did not sparkle with diamond-like stars, nor did a moon shed light upon the land. Pitch blackness seemed to be this night's preference. No matter. Angel could fight as well in the dark as in the light.

She gripped her sword, playing the weight. Had she not had her own weapon, she might have needed more practice, more time. Kaiya had also brought a sword with her—the dagger she carried at her waist became a sword on demand.

But the time had come. Shodak was in the clearing, unaware of their awareness. He expected to find livestock and peaceful townsfolk— perhaps a dragon as well, for the stories of Callamoon's defender had made many rounds through Criseyde. Shodak might expect a visit from a dragon or a set of scare tactics, but did not expect a full-blown battle.

Angel vowed to give him the fight of his life.

The tinny call sounded again. Liquid battle ran through Angel's veins. Only one thought crossed her mind as her boots pounded the ground and air burned her lungs.

*Kill.*

Sword met flesh, and a moment later the Gueritac lay on the ground, gasping in pain as she leapt over his body to insert her sword into another fae's chest. Two successes, two kills. But her fellow-fighters seemed worse off than she. A familiar voice cried out in pain. Dread settled in her stomach. If only there were light...She glanced at Faelan's trillium ring, the heliodor in the center catching her attention. She placed her concentration in its direction and prayed for a response.

The crystallized sunshine sublimed into the illumination of the battlefield. The work of a moment gave light to the battle and offered the good a helping hand. The Son's gift.

She blinked her shock away. She had no time to inquire of *how* it had worked, though she had been certain it would. Her sword needed to taste blood in order to be quenched, and all other swords in her sight needed the same thing. She did not plan to quench anyone else's sword.

Then she saw it.

Shodak, dragging Mercy from a wagon, a knife held to her throat and terror in her eyes. Too many creatures separated them, too many creatures stood in her way. But she *had* to save Mercy, and none of her allies seemed aware of her sister's plight. She *had* to save Mercy.

She summoned her magic, digging as deep as the depths of her power would allow, and she let the magic burst forth in an explosion of blackness equal to the night which surrounded their patch of light. The light began to dim as Angel's vision faded. The magic depleted her reserves and exhausted all her senses. Then something unexpected happened.

It exploded.

"Angel!"

Faelan's voice! She had to go to him, get him to help her sister. But she could not rise from where she had fallen and her vision was fading. The din of battle seemed to have disappeared into the searing pain of a volcano's fire, broiling her within its glowing orange heat. All she could sense was a blurry elfin face as it said "I tried, Angel. I tried to save you."

She knew. She knew his loyalty and goodness. She knew his love. She knew he had tried. He had not failed.

But she had.

# Chapter Eighteen

Words invaded the void like random pieces of a shattered looking-glass. Voices of uncertain origin cleared and faded. Some voices seemed familiar, others stranger than a flower in the dead of winter. But the shards of conversation haunted her, sending her tumbling through the darkness with only her ears to guide her direction. Or did she imagine the voices also?

*"Is she alright?"*

*"She needs to wake up soon."*

*"She is lovely."*

*"Angel, you must wake up. Angel..."*

She knew the last voice. She had never heard its sweetness before and she desired never to be out of its reach again. She wished to hear His voice again and again...forever and ever. Maybe, if she obeyed His words, she would get what she desired.

She opened her eyes.

Bright lights bobbed up and down, around and over. Warm air carried cool breezes to her cheek. An elf looked down, his blurred face seeming familiar. She reached to touch it and felt its smooth cheek. She placed her hand on his chest and felt a steady heartbeat beneath her palm.

"I did not think there would be heartbeats in heaven."

"They made an exception for me."

The laugh and voice could not be mistaken. She attempted to sit up, but vertigo caused her to fall back onto her pillow. Her vision still had not cleared, but she blinked at the figure and rubbed her hands over her face. "I am...I thought I was dead."

"I thought so too." He said. He lifted her off the mattress and leaned her upright against the wall.

The movement caused temporary dizziness, but the unclear images soon returned to their rightful places. But no matter how she tried, she could not see clearly. She could make out Faelan's form, but she could not guess what he held until he pressed it to her lips and said "Drink this, Angel. You have been out for two days and you will dehydrate soon."

She raised her hands to take the cup, but he did not release it. T'was best that way. Her hands shook like windblown reeds. She would have spilled three-quarters of the contents had he given it to her.

Two cups of sweet milk and three of clabbered milk were offered after the initial glass of water and all six cups were consumed by a grateful stomach. Faelan sat the cup aside after this and touched her cheek.

"Angel, you have not stopped squinting your eyes. Can't you see me?"

Angel shook her head. "I can see only basic shapes and blurs of color."

"I wondered." He said. "When Kaiya filled your other half, I wondered about your eyesight. No elf has gray eyes, yet she said she had to leave yours that way. Hold on, I'll repair your vision."

The words he spoke prompted her to ask questions, but his movements kept her silent. His hand reached up, his fingertips touching her tired eyelids and offering a rested sensation. Then bright, colorful light pulsed through her vision. When she opened her eyes again, she saw nothing but Faelan's face.

His eyes had dark circles beneath them and the whites had been tinged green from lack of sleep, but his smile was radiant, filling her with joy and hope and beauty.

"Good, they're still gray." He said, his hand resting upon her cheek. "Can you see?"

She nodded. "You are tired. You must sleep."

"Yes, Angel." He laughed. "I will sleep, for your sake. But you must sleep too."

"Nay." Angel said. "I do not wish to sleep."

But her eyes ached to be closed again and the liquids she had consumed sat pleasantly in her stomach, weighing her conscious down and bringing her closer to sleep with every moment she stayed awake.

"*You must sleep...*"

# Chapter Nineteen

Though sleep wins all battles to avoid it, it does not remain master over its subject for long. When Angel again found the strength to overthrow sleep's power, blurs of blue and yellow met her sight. These images cleared into two faeries.

She sat up, having found the strength to do so, and looked at the two. "My companion. Jas. Where is Faelan? Where is Mercy?"

"Angel." The fairy said uncomfortably. "There is much to explain."

"Is Mercy alright? She did not die, did she? Did I strike her with my magic?"

"Calm down." Jas said. "You needn't be afraid. Mercy is in far better condition than you."

This news caused such total relief that she collapsed against the wall. She looked again at Jas, who seemed to have better answers than her companion, and inquired of her sister's location. No sooner had she done so than he burst with laughter. "She's right in front of you!"

Her companion's cheeks turned a lovely pink color. "Yes, sister. The reason I could not speak my name—the reason I feared speaking—I had to see you inside the castle. But I could not let you know I was there."

Angel's head began to throb and she pushed her fingers into her temples. For the first time she became sensible of some pleasing changes. Her ears had grown pointier and smoother. The fingers with which she massaged her head were soft and uncalloused. Her back fit flat against the wall. No wings separated her back from the wooden planks of the cottage wall. Faelan had said something, when he fixed her vision, about no elf having gray eyes. He had not meant her, had he?

Jas recovered himself from laughter. "It is due to the Law of Blood. You see, you struck who you *thought* to be Shodak, but I had killed him several hours earlier. The creature you struck was someone I had disguised as Shodak. You struck Mercy."

The ensuing explanation revealed many unknown facts and half-truths which Jakie told her. Mercy *had*, at first, refused to let Jas take her place. But when he showed her why he would not be discovered, she agreed to leave, and he changed her image into Shodak's. How he changed their images also warranted explanation and he revealed that, like Ranger, he was of the Shape-shifter Clan. Being of the blue wing, however, he had far more power than the king.

"The reason for all of this," Jas said, "deals with the Law of Blood. It is a magical bond that prevents faeries from harming their blood-relatives. Because your magic struck Mercy, and Kaiya had placed some of your magic in her veins, your magic backfired and destroyed your faerie half."

"But," he continued "it is a *magical* bond. Your elfin half, being non-magical, was unaffected. Mercy's elfin half was obliterated. Kaiya and Jakie used magic to heal the damage in time enough to save your lives. Jakie would not have been able to do anything, of course, had she not had the trillium insignia on her hand."

"But why the circuitous route?" Angel inquired. "Why not just tell us what to do instead of putting us through all of this?"

"For one reason only: him."

Angel followed the direction of Jas' pointing finger, her eyes landing upon Faelan's sleeping form. "What do you infer?"

"If you had not met him, you would still be scarred, if you had not been imprisoned alongside him, you would not realize your mistakes. If you had not met him, you never would have fallen in love."

Angel growled at Jas. "You know nothing regarding myself and Faelan. You cannot."

"Just as Jakie cannot see the world from her castle? You know better than that, Angel. Now there is no cause for you to separate yourself from him."

She growled again, but he paid no heed to her hostile expressions. He simply kissed Mercy's forehead and left the room.

Mercy watched him leave and turned back to Angel, her eyes glowing. "He knows you, Angel. You cannot hide from him."

"I can hide from no one." She said. "You, Kaiya, Faelan...all of you are padparadscha. Soon there will not be a soul who cannot look through me and see what little heart I have beneath."

Mercy did not respond to this. She said only "You can no longer be mistaken for Dark Angel. What will you do now?"

"I know not. Perhaps I shall do as Heart and Blood do, teaching towns how to defend against the Gueritac. It is better, I suppose, to sear off the head of the serpent than to pluck the scales one by one."

Mercy smiled. "That is exactly what Faelan believed you would say. He said he would follow you there."

Angel scowled. "He shall not! He will settle happily with a pretty elfin woman somewhere in a lovely forest. He shall not follow my path of pain as you and Edan did."

Mercy stood and walked to the side of the room, then returned to her chair to grasp Angel's hand. "It caused pain, it caused destruction, but have you not seen it as rewarding also? When we took the irons off the wrists of creatures who thought themselves bound for life—did it not touch your heart?"

"I felt little from the first Gueritac's death to the moment I released Faelan from his shackles. The only thing I felt in between was admiration for you."

"For me? You are not serious, sister. Please, do not pain me."

"I know your goodness too well. It is like Faelan's. I deserve neither of your notice."

"But you do! I know I cannot convince you on this point, but try yourself to believe it. You are my sister. I love you. Faelan, you must awake! Tell my sister her virtues, for I am too close for her to believe my words."

The elf groaned and rubbed his eyes. Angel protested and asked him to return to sleep, but he seemed overjoyed to find her awake. She tried to discourage his delight by uttering her faults and her past cruelties, but he stopped her half-sentence.

"And what of my temper? My stubbornness? Do you count none of this in your favor? Surely I find no fault in you that cannot be countered by my own. We would make a perfect pair, touring the elfin tribes; you teaching the weapons and I teaching the Word. Our obstinacy will be the Gueritac's most fearsome enemy."

Did he truly wish this path? Was his desire to be a wanderer among the tribes? If he had not told her of his being a missionary, she would have refused him again and again. But if he wished to wander, would it be so much more trouble to wander with her? Was it what he desired?

Mercy coughed. "Angel, please excuse me from the room. I must get some willow tea. My head feels like a cracked walnut."

With that short speech Mercy departed from the room. Faelan looked after her and laughed as the door closed. "She is a gem, Angel. A lovely heliodor, with yellow hair and wing. Jas loves her dearly."

"Yes," she said "I am surprised *you* do not love her dearly."

"Now why do say that?" He asked. Then he shook his head. "No need to answer, Angel. You believed I would like her far better than you. But you did not take into account preference. A heliodor is perfect for Jas—bright and sunny with the clear innocence of a flawless gem. But look at you. Look at your skin. It is the same shade of green as mine. We are emeralds—foggy and flawed, but offering our colors as ornaments to glorify jewels of greater worth."

She felt warmth. The warmth spread from her cheeks to her toes and finally she allowed their corners to turn up in a smile. "You are strange."

"I know." He said. His palms held her cheeks, his thumbs resting on the points of her ears. "I am a missionary. And so are you. When you're stronger, we'll set out. I have some business in the last village I 'left,' so we shall go there before anywhere else."

"But what shall I do in the meantime?" She asked. "What can I do until I recover my strength?"

At this he raised an eyebrow. "If Kaiya had her way, we'd be married before sundown...but I think the ceremony would bore you. I could have Mercy read as she did before. Or I could talk until you decide the ceremony would bore you less."

"Then talk." Angel said. "The sooner you bore me, the sooner the ceremony may take place."

# Chapter Twenty

The wagon's wheels ceased turning as the clearing broke. She leaned against his shoulder. She listened, and her attention was rewarded with words.

"It has been four weeks, Angel. I wonder what happened to them. What has happened since the Gueritac stole me away?"

"Kaiya sent them food. Jakie surely would have sent us away sooner had she feared their safety."

"Yes, I know." He said. "But I still see the flames."

Not another word was spoken. Faelan snapped the horses into motion. They drew nearer to the village. The air became thinner. Their hearts beat faster. A wolf appeared at the outside of the village. Faelan breathed a sigh of relief.

"Tala is here."

Angel urged him to push the horses faster. He did so but it was unnecessary, for the wolf bounded over and hopped upon the sacks of grain, howling as it reached the top. Then the wolf looked down, the face changing to that of a fairy.

"It has taken you long enough." Said the wolf-girl. "What kept you? This pretty thing, perhaps?"

"Perhaps." Faelan replied. "But what can you expect of a bride and groom? You were a bride not long ago."

Tala laughed. "I speak only in jest...Come, the villagers are anxious to see you. They have been hiding an object of uncertain existence for the past month. I have been here over three weeks but they refuse to show it to anyone until you returned. I begin to doubt it is anything but a decision on which of the single ladies have first dibs. They will be so very disappointed."

It took but a moment to reach the village. The villagers gathered around. They had not, Angel knew, expected to recover the grain and tools they lost. But they had also not expected to see their tribesmen again. Shock gave in to delight in an eye-blink, and all began asking questions and inquiring after the load the healer had brought.

With little time wasted, Faelan began giving orders to several male elves. Angel took it upon herself to aid with the smaller items. Utensils, knives and weapons passed through Angel's hands, and as she worked, she heard a familiar voice. She glanced and saw an elf of Faelan's age accepting a sack of grain from Faelan's hand.

Angel knew him. How could she forget the elf who commended Faelan? The elf now had something to say of her, it seemed.

"Who's she?"

"Her?" Faelan said. "Her name is Angel. She's my wife."

"Wife!"

"Is it so strange that I could fall in love? Now do take care of that sack. You'll strain your back if you hold it much longer."

The elf obeyed, but returned insisting he be allowed to help Faelan unload. Faelan thanked him, but asked him to assist Angel. The elf reluctantly agreed, but was proficient in his help and promptly began a conversation with Angel.

She tried to be friendly. In every manner of the word, she tried. But her throat could not lose the hoarseness it had acquired and the shortness of her sentences caused the appearance of hostility. Still, the elf remained kind and she learned much from his conversation. She learned his name— Mikad—and many things about Faelan's travels. He even managed to speak a few words in her praise. Whether he was sincere, she could not say.

"Now come," Tala said as they finished. "My curiosity is unreasonably riled—you must show us the thing you saved for Faelan."

"Yes," Mikad said, addressing Angel. "If you allow me to part you from your husband a moment, you shall soon see what I found."

Angel watched the two elves—and several others—enter a hut. She stood at the door only a few moments more before entering. She could not bear to be away from her husband any longer.

The sight, hastily taken in, caused her to run to his side, her attention on his tears alone. But the moment she came near he embraced her and pointed to the book Mikad held in his hands.

It was a book of songs and poetry, things which would never have provoked such tears from Faelan. The songs, in fact, did not matter at all. Only the thing which had been kept flat and dry between its pages interested either of them.

"I found it when I returned." Mikad said. "I was searching for anything the Gueritac had left. I think it fell from the pages when the Gueritac picked it up—long before they burned it. Not five hours later, Tala and Seff came with supplies. An omen, I suppose. But it is yours again. Take it."

Faelan took the delicate flower and held it in his fingers. Angel touched the yellowed petals and dark leaves. She knew the significance of the flower without being told.

"If we return to Callamoon," she said "We might return it to Kaiya."

"We might." He replied. "But she no longer needs it. Nor do I. It's lovely, but its meaning is far more important. This is the reason Jakie sent us here."

Faelan squeezed her shoulder. *I heal you, you heal me.*

"Callamoon is the perfect place for this flower." He said. "It is a place of healing—it would be among its own kind."

"Yes." Angel agreed. "It shall go to Callamoon."

So, the fate of the trillium decided, Mikad insisted that if the flower must be taken to Callamoon *he* would do it for them. But as the elf left on his errand both the healer and the warrior knew that if he did return, it would not be for long. The circuitous course and the dangers of the path notwithstanding, all creatures that embarked on the journey returned with their strings pulled and their future decided. They returned healed or battered, broken or mended. Everyone did.

No one could escape the road to Callamoon.

# About the Author

Crystal grew up deep in the woods of Maine where she spent most of her spare time reading great works from other authors. But finding books about fairies that suited her taste being nearly impossible, she soon endeavored to create the most perfect work of that type in her ability...and she hasn't stopped writing since.

www.ingramcontent.com/pod-product-compliance
Lightning Source LLC
Chambersburg PA
CBHW070753120626
46557CB00002B/574